A Cat's
Judgement

Mr Perkins lays down the law

A Cat's Judgement

Mr Perkins lays down the law

Written and illustrated by

Suzanne Stephenson

Also by the author

Bearswood End
Mr Perkins Takes Charge
The World According To Patrick White

'Forever Waste' a light romantic comedy

Introduction

Cats have not always had a good press, although the ancient Egyptians had a cat god Bastet. While in Medieval times cats were often associated with Satan and black magic, Queen Victoria who was a keeper of cats, and the writer Mark Twain did much to restore the reputation of cats. There have been several cats who have lived at the seat of government, namely in Downing Street, London. Who is to say a cat could not bring his or her beneficial influence to bear on the judicial system.

Chapter 1

District Judge Nicholas Blyton had spent years dreaming of being a full-time District Judge and now he was appointed to such a post he was absolutely terrified. Although the Judicial Appointments people had tried hard to find him a post close to his current home, it was not to be. He would have to get used to sitting in a court he did not know. His family agreed that they should all move house, so he did not have to find some bedsit and be all on his own during the week. For that he was very grateful, but the sale and purchase had yet to complete so he would need to live in lodgings on a temporary basis.

He would miss his wife Danya, his daughter Maria, his son Harry, and the family dog, a Red Setter called Jasper. He knew he would not be apart from them for too long. Then his wife who had transferrable skills, namely bookkeeping would need to find another job and his children would have to get used to their new school. The consolation was also that they would only be less than an hour by car from family members, and his new house was an improvement on their current home. He had also been fortunate in locating what he thought sounded like very suitable temporary quarters. "The Judges' Lodgings Guest House B & B" had indeed been "Judges' Lodgings" many years in the past but were now a guest house in walking distance from the court. The advertising not only extolled its oak panelling and atmosphere but referred to its generous breakfast and evening meals. Each room was said to be spacious and boast a large desk with space to work for the business traveller, free Wi-Fi, and plenty of wardrobe space. It had a car park of its own and was in walking distance from the court and had views from its garden of the municipal park.

The city to which he was locating was not just some tourist area, although it did have an old centre. There was a fine cathedral which had its origins in Norman times but had been much refurbished and extended in the early 19th century with some more recent restoration work which brought out its best features. The local information pamphlet told him there was a close of old houses next to the cathedral which housed the bishop and his staff and a couple of alleyways in that area that featured some Tudor houses. Nearby there was a large city square which was bordered by the Georgian Town Hall, and a Victorian era theatre and art gallery. Just behind the Town Hall was the Grammar School which was hemmed in by other buildings and which did not have its sports field in situ.

Unfortunately, the main city centre shopping and commercial area was a nineteen sixties development which replaced shops of an earlier era. The large nineteen seventies Combined Court building housed the Magistrates' Court, the Crown Court, and the County Court and had a very small concrete yard behind it. There was a convenient but ugly multi-storey car park next door to it on one side and a large city centre pub on the other side. A few streets of older Georgian and Victorian houses which included "The Judges' Lodgings B & B", a private medical clinic, a fine dining restaurant, and an antiques' centre, remained near the city centre and the local park. There was another commercial centre complete with office blocks, a chain hotel or two and more shops out near the railway station.

The city had also swallowed up two former villages which had grown and spread during the industrial revolution and there was now a large housing estate between the two former villages. There were a couple of parks, a couple of industrial areas, and a large out of town shopping centre which also housed a multi-plex cinema and the football arena. Cheek by jowl with the out-of-town shopping centre were four blocks of hideous high-rise flats and another housing estate. The city's original hospital had long ago been demolished and the main hospital now sat beside the out-of-town shopping centre.

It was in many areas other than the old centre a practical rather than attractive city. It had some pleasant countryside with flowing, undulating hills surrounding it with some pretty villages. Nick had chosen the nearest village for his home. He hoped the seemingly pleasant surroundings to the former Edwardian vicarage would be some compensation to his family for the move. And he would be able to take Jasper, the Red Setter for nice walks. As well as farmland where cows and sheep could be spotted grazing there were woodlands with a network of public footpaths. He mused that he might obtain another canine friend for Jasper, or perhaps a cat or two and a handful of hens to peck away at the bottom of the garden.

The wind had seemingly buffeted him up the motorway to his new city. He drove into the car park that fine windy afternoon feeling the journey had taken no time at all. As he got out of the car a voice said loudly and insistently, "Miaow."

He looked down and saw a slightly bedraggled black cat with yellow eyes. The cat rubbed against his legs. Nick said,

"Hello, do you live here?"

The cat purred and continued to rub against him. Nick had grown up with cats in the house and his parents had a large Tabby called Tiger with whom he seemed to have an affinity. Nick lifted his suitcase out of his car and headed to reception. He pushed open the front door of "The Judges' Lodgings B & B" and went inside. The black cat slipped inside the building, between his legs.

The reception area reflected something of the building's past use, with tasteful panelling and engravings of judges from past eras. The smiling proprietor of the guest house greeted him.

"Hello," she said, "I am Vicky Poletree… you must be my new guest."

"I'm Nick Blyton, I have a booking for a few weeks although I might have to extend it if my house move is delayed. The booking is for a large room with en suite facilities, desk and sitting area."

As Nick dealt with the formalities the black cat rubbed around his legs and purred loudly.

Vicky said,

"If you need anything during your stay, just ask me or my daughter Natasha who lives here. We are here all the time," she looked a little sad. "Used to be Natasha, Jim, and I but sadly Jim passed away last year due to leukaemia. Tasha and I just soldier on…"

"Well, it seems a delightful place," said Nick, "and with a lovely friendly cat too."

Vicky peered over the desk and said,

"He's not mine." The cat purred very loudly. Vicky said, "He makes me think of a cat Jim had when we were first married. We started with a cat and dog. They both lived goodly lives and the cat lived until he was nineteen and we seriously thought of getting another one but then Jim was ill…"

Nick noticed the collecting tins for Cats' Protection and a local dog rescue centre on the desk. The cat looked inscrutable and continued purring. A young girl of about eighteen appeared. She smiled shyly from behind the desk. Nick noticed she was wearing a hearing aid.

"This is Tasha," said Vicky.

"How do you do, I'm Nick Blyton," said Nick, speaking slowly and rather loudly.

"Hello, welcome," said Tasha. "There is no need to shout at me. I have a little hearing one side and I can lip-read, especially when people speak clearly."

Nick nodded with embarrassment and felt himself go red. Tasha spotted the cat who strangely no longer looked bedraggled.

"He's gorgeous," she said. "Did you bring him with you? We allow the occasional well-behaved dog, but we have never had a guest bring a cat."

"No, not guilty!" laughed Nick. The cat jumped onto the counter next to the collection tins and purred even more loudly.

"My, what a purr, it's like an engine," said Nick.

"Purry, purry pussy. I can feel his purr vibrate," said Tasha stroking the cat.

"Perhaps he's called Mr Purr-kins!" joked Vicky. "I'll find him some milk and some chicken once I've shown you to your room."

The black cat looked suitably inscrutable. His yellow eyes shone like glowing embers in a grate. He followed Nick and Vicky to Nick's room and sat in the corridor just outside as if supervising the humans.

"This is number eight of our eight rooms, dinner is at seven if that's okay?" said Vicky as she handed Nick the key which was attached to a key ring with a metal disc which had an "8" one side and a faint engraving of a judge's head the other side. Nick expressed his satisfaction with the room and smiled as he saw the black cat follow Vicky back down the corridor, as he was closing the door.

Nick began unpacking his belongings. This involved making a couple of trips to the car to collect further bags. On the second occasion he spotted the black cat again, this time sat in an open side doorway to the building. Vicky was bent over talking to him. There was a lot of loud purring.

"I think he's definitely decided he likes it here," laughed Nick. "And from the purring he really is a Mr Perkins."

"If he keeps hanging around here," said Vicky, "I will have to make some enquiries as to whether anyone has lost a cat."

She paused and sounded wistful. "This is the fire-exit door. The panel at the bottom covers the old cat-flap which was there for my old cat."

Nick smiled. He liked that his landlady liked animals. The whole business with the cat was a good distraction as he would otherwise have dwelled on how lonely and nervous he was feeling. By the time he had unpacked and had a long telephone call with his family it was nearly six o'clock. He sat down on the bed and kicked off his shoes having decided to have a short rest before dinner... perhaps he would read some leaflets about the city left on his desk. Before he knew it, he was asleep. He woke with a start.

"Miaow," said a loud insistent voice.

He looked at his watch. It said five to seven.

"How did you get in here?" he asked. The cat looked suitably inscrutable. He noticed the door was slightly ajar although he thought he had shut it.

"Well, I best go down to dinner," he said. The cat purred.

He pulled on his shoes and quickly readied himself to go downstairs. The cat followed him along the corridor and downstairs. He looked about him and found a white door with a sign saying, "Dining Room". He pushed open the door and spoke to the cat,

"Not sure you are allowed in there."

"Miaow," was the response from the black cat who jumped up onto the nearby reception desk.

The room housed eight tables, most of which had two chairs at each of them. There was wood panelling until about waist height and then the walls were painted a tasteful cream. There were a number of Hogarth style prints in gilt frames showing eighteenth century court scenes. The room was lit by a chandelier style electric light. The sash windows gave a pleasant view out onto the garden and the trees in the park beyond it. There was a pair of French windows as well, centrally situated which led into a small conservatory which in turn had doors leading to the garden. The conservatory had a collection of wicker armchairs and a central coffee table.

There was a small menu card on each table in the dining room where he was presumably going to have his meal.

Tasha came out of a side door and gestured to a table set for one person. There were a handful of other diners present in the room. He picked up the menu and read it. It said:

"Starters

Tomato soup or smoked salmon.

Mains

Roast Chicken, smoked salmon salad, or pasta with a herby tomato sauce.

Dessert

Cheesecake, peach sorbet, or cheeseboard
Apple or orange juice, tea, coffee".

As he thought about his own choices, he could not stop himself wondering if the black cat might not like the leftovers. That thought continued to invade his consciousness as he ate his meal, so much so that he found himself secreting a small piece of chicken in a napkin and placing it in his pocket during the meal. It was a satisfying meal. The guesthouse did not have an alcohol licence. He thought he might ask if once in a while he could bring a bottle of wine in with him, but most nights juice and tea or coffee would be quite satisfactory.

After dinner he found the cat was still sitting at the reception desk looking as if he owned the premises.

"I'm going outside for a breath of air," he said as if addressing a person. "Want to come outside?"

"Miaow," said the black cat and followed him out of the doors. He reached into his pocket and sat himself down on a bench close to the front door. He unwrapped the piece of chicken and gave it to the cat who soon made it disappear and then purred loudly.

"You are very friendly," said Nick. "I wonder if someone has lost you."

The cat looked inscrutable but purred. Nick sat for a while digesting his dinner.

"Ah, well," he later said, "time to go indoors."

The cat followed him inside and took up his place on the reception desk. Vicky appeared.

"You know I've never seen him down this road before. I have asked next-door, and they know nothing about him either," she said. "If he is still hanging around in the morning, I will put a post on social media. I still do wonder what his name is…"

The black cat purred.

"Blackie, Tibbles, Jet, Tommy…" she tried in turn. He stood up and hissed and arched his back at each of the names she tried. He sat down again once she finished trying names. Nick stroked the cat's head and he started to purr again.

"That's a very loud purr," he said, "eh, Mr Purr-kins?" The purring got louder.

"Mr Perkins it is, for the time being," laughed Vicky. Nick went upstairs to his room.

He thought he was not going to sleep but he dropped off quickly, dreaming of a coal black cat with amber eyes who purred throughout his slumbers. Once again, he woke up with a jolt. He could hear his bedroom door rattling.

"Who's there?" he called out.

"Miaow," was the loud insistent reply.

As he was only clad in pyjama bottoms, Nick only opened the door very slightly. The cat walked inside his room.

"Come to make sure I am not late?" he queried.

"Miaow," was the response. The cat climbed onto his bed and lay there purring.

Suitably showered and dressed, Nick made his way downstairs a short time later, followed by his feline companion. The cat sat himself at reception while he drank some coffee and tried to eat some toast and marmalade. He felt a shiver go down his spine when he thought of his new job and his hands felt very clammy. After struggling to eat breakfast he went to his room to collect his briefcase and his thoughts. He reassured himself he had many years' experience as a lawyer, and he had also over five years' experience as a Deputy District Judge. Plucking up his courage he went downstairs again.

"Oh, Mr Perkins," he said to the black cat who was stretched across the reception desk, "I hope you will bring me luck." The black cat purred and looked inscrutable.

Vicky appeared and said affably," See you later."

Nick plucked up his courage and headed for the front door.

The black cat remained on the desk for a few minutes.

"I'll have to make some inquiries about you," said Vicky tickling the cat's chin. Then she went into the dining room to help Tasha clear away the breakfast things.

There was a flurry of other guests coming downstairs and going outside. Some paused to look at the black cat. Eventually the black cat took himself outside as the door swung open for one of the guests.

Nick stopped at a newsagent's shop on the corner of the street. He bought a newspaper, and a juice and some biscuits and an apple, which he might have during the day at court. He did not realise that while he was in the shop the black cat had all but caught up with him and was following in the shadows as he walked to the court.

It was only a few minutes before Nick found himself outside the Combined Court. He debated about whether he should find the backdoor, but as he would need a security pass to even walk through the car park entrance, he decided to head for the main entrance. He was totally unaware of the black cat in the shadows who was carefully surveying the scene, and who after a few minutes took himself to a narrow alleyway by the pub next door which would lead him to a beer garden and thence onwards to the yard and car park behind the court. As Nick was passing through the main entrance, the black cat sat hidden from view under some large commercial waste bins in the court car park.

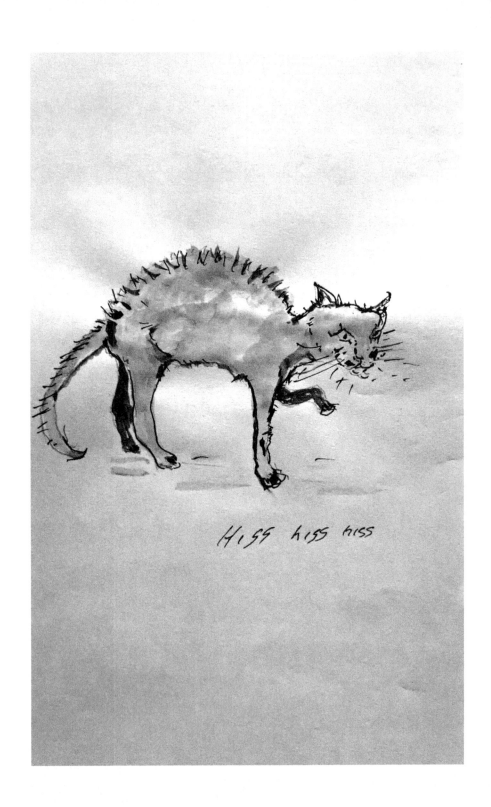

HiSS hiss hiss

Chapter 2

Despite the fact the Combined Court had been built in the nineteen seventies and was supposedly maintained with public money, it had a careworn look to it. The royal crest was still there outside, but something was amiss with the lettering which now read "Ombined Ourt" as the letter "C" had dropped off and repairs had yet to be completed. Nick Blyton entered through the front door and was immediately confronted by the most bored looking security men he had ever encountered. There were two security arches ahead of him. He introduced himself,

"Fred," it's the new guy. Shall I still check him out?" said one guard to the other, as if he wasn't there.

"Yeah, Luke, do you think he'll last longer than the previous one?" came the reply.

"We'll have to check you out, sir," said Luke to Nick. "Should be easier when you get a pass."

Nick said that he understood. He wondered what happened to "the previous one". He didn't think it right to ask. However, as he passed through the arch Luke added,

"Oh and mind the buckets. Roof's leaking again."

Nick saw there was a line of three buckets. He looked up and noticed there was the odd drip coming down from the glass roof. When the court had opened no doubt, the users had welcomed the light and airy foyer created by having a high glass panelled roof to the area. Now, a passing shower was causing drips to plop down into the line of buckets. Nick wondered with trepidation what else awaited him.

"Where do I go from here?" he asked Luke.

"'ang on I'll radio the office to see if you are expected... sit there." He pointed to a bench in the corner away from the drips.

Of course he was expected, thought Nick, but he did as he was asked. A few minutes later a flustered looking, red-faced woman appeared. She proffered a hand,

"Hello, I'm Renee Rollwright the Delivery Manager for the Combined Court. I'm sorry you're welcome has not been better. Let me take you to my office. I've had a terrible morning. The lists have become all jumbled up, no-one has turned up to survey our leaks and the building maintenance manager advises that we have an infestation of mice. It seems so far, they have shredded half the contents of a stationery cupboard. God forbid they go for archived paper files or cabling." Her voice tailed off. Nick found himself being escorted through a usually locked door to the staff area of the court. They walked at speed through a general office and down a corridor until Renee pushed open a door and unannounced,

"Here it is! My humble abode."

She beckoned him to a chair. Nick sat down and looked around him. The room was small and windowless. There was a chair behind a desk and two other chairs. Various bits of electronic paraphernalia including a screen sat on the desk. There was one filing cabinet with what looked to be a couple of family photos on top of it. There was a large year planner on the wall with some scribbled words on it and a colourful calendar which bore the heading "Views of Tenerife". On a stool in a corner a kettle, two mugs and a jar of instant coffee were balanced precariously. Nick sincerely hoped his Chambers would be better than this.

"Would you like a drink?" asked Renee, gesturing to the kettle.

Nick shook his head. She pushed some untidy curls back from her face and said,

"Right. Welcome District Judge Blyton, and despite appearances you are very much welcome. I will sort out your security card in the next few days. Shortly I will give you a tour of the building. I have made sure you only have a shortish list today. I split the possession list, so you don't have to start until 11am. I am sure you will need time after our tour to sort out your judicial lap-top and other equipment. Then your list is not too long this afternoon. Hopefully at 4 o'clock you can join the staff and myself in the staff restroom for tea and biscuits and introductions to the team."

She paused, "Everything okay so far?"

Nick nodded. She continued.

"The court offices and areas for the public with counters are downstairs, plus a Citizen's Advice Bureau room, some seating areas with a cold drink machine and public toilets too. If you wonder why my room is not the best, I preferred that the staff had a large rest room. That meant we had to move the bailiff room and chief bailiff's office. Then we needed a room for our team leaders and two rooms for legal advisors. By the time we moved everyone round I was left with this."

She paused again and spoke.

"On the first floor we have three large courts, a collection of interview rooms and a large waiting area. On the second floor we have two District Judges' Chambers, a large courtroom, three Circuit Judges' Chambers, one interview room, and a small waiting area. On the third floor we have a small courtroom, a District Judges' Chambers, two magistrates' retiring rooms, the Jury suite and a small waiting area. There is a judicial dining room sandwiched in behind Court 2 on the first floor but gone are the days when we had caterers in the building. The canteen was ripped out years ago to create Court 4."

"Where will I be?" asked Nick.

"Chambers 3 on the third floor," was the reply.

"Now, the sitting patterns are a bit complicated too," continued Renee. "Their Honours Judge Hassan Shah KC and Bernard Woldborough are our permanent Circuit Judges, although each of them spends three months per year away from us at the Royal Courts of Justice. His Honour Judge Shah KC is the Designated Family Judge and His Honour Judge Woldborough is the Designated Civil Judge. They both of course do crime. We frequently have visits from His Honour Judge Stanley D'Artagnon KC. He has tickets for just about any type of work and is based at the circuit centre. The District Judges are District Judge Petunia Partington who is here most of the time, District Judge Roger Shadow who is with us two days a week, District Judge Laura Stolinska who also sits with us three days per fortnight and now, yourself. We fit the magistrates in when and where we can. We also have use of an old building just behind the Grammar School. It is a remnant of the old Magistrates' Court. It still has a courtroom and some rather antiquated toilets in it. Sometimes the magistrates sit at that court but sometimes it is useful for District Judge trials with more people than your Chambers can accommodate."

They talked about one or two more details and then Renee started the tour. As they bowled along the downstairs staff corridor at speed there was a piercing scream.

"That's probably just Netty, one of the ushers meeting some mice," she said, before calling out, "everything OK?"

A disembodied voice called out of a side room,

"No, it bloody isn't. They have got at the staff choccy biccy supply."

Renee called back, "I'll deal with it later. I have our new District Judge on a tour."

They eventually reached Nick's Chambers.

There were six rows of seats which could accommodate 4 or 5 on each row as long the litigants or witnesses were not portly. In front of the banks of seats were two tables side by side. There was a small, raised dais upon which rested a very new looking desk behind a panel. Behind the desk was a swivel chair. Behind the swivel chair was a panelled wall with the royal crest, and set to one side, was a door saying "Private". They opened a gate in the panel and squeezed through up onto the dais.

Renee opened the door marked "Private". There was a tiny room which housed a cupboard. On top of it sat a kettle and above it were four coat hooks. Squeezing past the cupboard Nick could see there was a small windowless room housing a toilet and washbasin.

Nick nodded. Somewhere his consciousness registered a distant "Miaow". Surely not? Nick noted the extreme narrowness of the desk and wondered how he would put anything much on it. Renee saw him peering at it and said,

"Ah, the desk." She looked embarrassed. "We have had various temporary transfers over the last two years. Seeing as you are supposed to be our permanent full-timer, we thought we would bring this Chambers up to date as it had not been refurbished for years. The dais, the desk and furniture are all new. The old furniture was basically a U-shape with the judge sitting in the middle. Frankly with some of the behaviour these days we were advised it was not a safe layout. We had the dais built but we didn't have a desk which fitted so the contractors said they would do it… we told them what was needed, and this is what we got…"

Her voice tailed off.

"I hope they didn't charge much," said Nick.

"£4000," said Renee almost in a whisper.

Nick was speechless.

While he was still gathering his thoughts Renee said, "Best leave you to it. Your usher Tracey will be along before your list starts."

Tracey indeed came along. She also helpfully brought him coffee at lunchtime since he only took a short break due to the needs of his list and did not go to meet his colleagues in the judges' dining room.

Most of the possession list he was to hear involved rent arrears and the proceedings were brought by social landlords. There were just one or two cases brought by private landlords towards the end of the list. He assumed that any applications to suspend evictions by the bailiff had gone over to another District Judge as these tended to be heard early. He had a bizarre sensation as the day wore on that there was an additional presence in his Chambers. Tracey was pleasant and polite and efficient. Initially nothing was particularly challenging. Eventually Tracey called on the last case, "Maltravers v Leroy".

A very short grumpy looking man with a tweed cap and a pipe came in followed by an extremely tall man with a Rastafarian bonnet.

Tracey said,

"Can you put your pipe out, sir, no smoking is allowed in the building and please remove your hat."

The man scowled. "What about his hat, then?" He pointed to the other man.

"I believe his head covering is part of his religion and culture," said Tracey.

"Blacks get it all their own way," said the grumpy man under his breath. Nick was surprised by both the pipe and the tweed cap since grumpy man would have had to pass through security.

"No racist comments under your breath," said Nick. The man mumbled a grudging apology.

The men sat a few feet apart behind the table.

"Now who is Enever Maltravers, the Claimant?" asked Nick.

"That's me," said the grumpy man.

"So, you must be Jeffrey Leroy, the Defendant," said Nick looking at the other man, who nodded and said, "Yes, sir."

"Now," said Nick, "this is a case under the Housing Act 1988. Mr Maltravers says he has served a section 8 notice relying on ground 14, nuisance or annoyance…"

"And a ruddy nuisance he is too," butted in Mr Maltravers scowling.

"Please wait until I speak to you," said Nick feeling irritated. "Now is there any dispute over the service of the notice or the format?" he turned to Mr Leroy.

"None at all," said Mr Leroy mildly. "I have had advice from the CAB.

It's not the formalities I dispute, but the facts. I can assure the court the accusations are untrue and it's not me who makes the noise he is complaining about…"

"Noisy, black…" interjected Mr Maltravers but he didn't get to finish his sentence. There was a sudden hiss, and then an "ouch" from Mr Maltravers and then a thud as the black cat jumped on Nick's desk. It was none other than the cat from the B&B now fixed in Nick's mind as "Mr Perkins".

"Where did that thing come from… it clawed me," said Mr Maltravers.

Nick stammered something about mice in the court building and added,

"It can't have clawed you because it could not have leaped from where you are sitting to my desk. It's too far."

Mr Perkins started purring and made himself comfortable on a corner of the desk.

"He's a lovely animal," said Mr Leroy. Mr Perkins' yellow eyes seemed to glow.

"What are you going to do about that thing?" interjected Mr Maltravers.

"Unless either of you have an allergy, nothing," said Nick confidently. "I need to get on with your case in the allotted time or it will have to be adjourned. I will sort out the cat later."

He couldn't believe what he had just said. Mr Maltravers indicated he didn't want an adjournment and Mr Leroy had no issue with the cat.

"Right, Mr Maltravers please explain what evidence you have and something of the layout of things as this may be relevant."

Mr Maltravers explained he was the owner of a semi-detached house divided into three small flats. Mr Leroy was the tenant of the top floor flat. Mr Maltravers lived next door with his wife on the ground and first floor of the house and his adult son had a studio flat on the second floor. Mr Maltravers' tenants had complained for some months about incessant noise at night in the form of the sound of drums. Mr Maltravers and his wife apparently had been kept awake as well. He indicated that he had given Mr Leroy numerous warnings, but the drumming noise had just continued.

"And," said Mr Maltravers, "as well as statements from my wife and others showing we can't get a decent night's sleep, I have diarised the noise… and I have recordings too!"

Nick said to Mr Leroy, "What do you say?"

"As I have tried to tell Mr Maltravers it cannot be me," said Mr Leroy. "For six nights out of every ten I am working a night shift at the hospital as a porter… the neighbours will say they hate the noise, but they won't say it's me… we get on okay."

Mr Maltravers was muttering under his breath, but Mr Perkins seemed to hiss at him.

Nick said, "And what about the four nights you are there?"

Mr Leroy replied, "Well, Judge I have to use earplugs to get a decent night's sleep, but there is nothing I can do about the vibration."

"Well," said Nick, "if it's not you who is it?"

"It's embarrassing, Judge," Mr Leroy started speaking, with Mr Maltravers initially looking triumphant, "I don't want to stir up trouble. And I would have thought Mr Maltravers would work it out eventually."

"Who is it?" said Nick.

"Well, it's his son, of course. The boy's been all over social media about entering some drumming competition. I didn't want to spoil things for the lad," said Mr Leroy wearily. "I can show you on my phone."

Mr. Maltravers looked thunderstruck, "It can't be. Surely… I thought he was studying for some engineering exams up there. This must be a lie… Someone like him would say that."

Nick asked for details about the social media accounts concerned and soon found the details on his judicial laptop.

Nick asked Mr Maltravers, "Can you raise the subject of the noise with your son?"

Mr Maltravers mumbled something about his son talking mainly to his mother.

"Well," said Nick, "it seems to me that the two of you might benefit from an adjournment for a couple of weeks. Mr Maltravers you might wish to investigate if your son has made the noise, and perhaps assist him in finding somewhere else to practice. It seems Mr Leroy will be able to put up matters in defence very much contesting the allegations. I will ask the court service to signpost you both to some mediation and in a couple of weeks' time you can tell me if this really needs a trial or if you are going to try and settle your differences."

He indicated that the hearing was over. Mr Perkins sat up and peered at Mr Maltravers and Mr Leroy with an enigmatic expression as they shuffled out.

Tracey reappeared and started to ask if he was ready to go and meet the staff, but then she saw Mr Perkins.

"What a lovely cat," she said. Mr Perkins purred. "Did you bring him in?"

Nick replied, "Not on purpose, he's a stray who seems to have taken a liking to the B&B and me. He must have followed me here and slipped indoors somehow."

Tracey looked doubtful, "Well, we could do with him 'cos of the mice in the building," she added.

Nick said that he would leave him in Chambers while he went to meet the staff. Mr Perkins stretched himself across the desk as he left to go and take tea and biscuits with the staff. Soon his mind was whirring as he met all the ushers. There was Tracey, Terry, Terri, Tarny, Tilly, Theresa and Anjelica. He met team leaders and Clerks and bailiffs. District Judge Petunia Partington and His Honour Judge Woldborough had joined the gathering too.

"We hoped to meet you at lunchtime," said Petunia.

Nick explained he had been rather busy with his list. Petunia and Bernard Woldborough seemed affable enough.

"Well try to get to the dining room at least once a week," he said. "It's useful to play catch-up with what's going on. For example, we have this rodent problem in the building. I was doing a particularly sensitive hearing and blow me if two mice ran across my clerk's desk! Fortunately, Megan my clerk is a calm person... but the witness screamed and briefly we had uproar."

Petunia said, "There is a rumour that a cat has got into the building."

Nick explained about the stray cat who had become named Mr Perkins following him into the building.

"Well," said Bernard, "Roger will hate him, but I think it would be a good thing if he makes a habit of visiting."

However, when Nick went up to his Chambers to collect his belongings, Mr Perkins was nowhere to be found. He wondered if he would see him again.

Chapter 3

Nick need not have worried about seeing his newfound friend Mr Perkins again. When he returned to "The Judges' Lodging B&B" there was Mr Perkins lying across the reception desk as if he had never left. Vicky Poletree greeted him with a smile.

"He seems to have made himself thoroughly at home," she said. "I have asked around the neighbourhood and no-one is missing a cat. He is so friendly, and Tasha loves him. I just need to make sure he doesn't get into any areas he shouldn't for food hygiene reasons. Or near anyone who has an allergy."

She spoke as if she wanted the cat to move in permanently. Nick smiled. He liked Mr Perkins' presence too. He felt the distraction of the cat's behaviour had given him more confidence. He was able to phone his family and tell them he was settling in at the court. He was not sure where the cat spent the night, but sure enough Mr Perkins walked with him to the court in the morning, even waiting outside the newsagent's while he bought a newspaper and some refreshments. When he reached the court, this time Nick was able to use the car park and staff entrances. Mr Perkins simply slipped inside with him. By the time he reached his Chambers his feline friend was nowhere to be seen.

Nick spent the morning dealing with some matrimonial financial cases, and feeling a little drained, nonetheless felt he should make his way to the judges' dining room. He looked about him.

There was District Judge Petunia Partington who greeted him warmly. An attractive woman in her early forties, perhaps some of her good looks had come from her Ghanian mother. Petunia was the product of a half English half Spanish barrister father and her barrister mother. It was inevitable she would do something in the law. Settled now with her husband Joe Partington, an acoustic engineer, on the outskirts of town, the couple had one child Milton, who was a constant worry to her and caused her to bite her nails to the quick. She had taken him to paediatricians, psychologists and counsellors to no real avail. All she could discover was that he had mild traits of being on the autism spectrum, but otherwise "You have a very healthy lively little boy".

Lively as he was at times, he also seemed a bit of a loner, like the time when he had climbed onto the Primary School roof with his book. "Just wanted a bit of peace to do some reading," he said. Like the time when he had run away from Sunday School and had somehow got into the Fire Station and smuggled himself onto a fire-engine. "Just wanted to see something more interesting." Other times he would be quiet to the point of being sullen, hiding away in his room with his books. Having started Secondary School this school year, he had not seemingly made any new friends. Thus far his behaviour had not been too bad, but the school were concerned that he was overly quiet.

His Honour Judge Woldborough greeted Nick. "Glad you could make it," he said.

Bernard Woldborough was a tall man in his early fifties with sandy grey hair and when he smiled his blue eyes would twinkle. Not that he smiled that often, preferring to cultivate a serious demeanour. His children were young adults who had flown the nest, and his wife Wendy was the administrator of a local hospice. The staff all thought well of him, and he had a reputation as a fair and compassionate judge. Once he was in a social gathering, they knew he could be warm and convivial and had a wry sense of humour.

Bernard Woldborough introduced Nick to the other judges present. His Honour Judge Hassan Shah KC stretched out his hand to make a friendly greeting as did District Judge Laura Stolinska.

His Honour Judge Shah KC was a short dapper man. He was reputed to have the most precise knowledge of family law anywhere on the circuit. Practitioners feared him, because he knew exactly what every rule and every family statute said and his memory of caselaw was encyclopaedic. Litigants often were unsure what to make of him before they had been in his court; the odd racist was soon brought down to size because His Honour Judge Shah KC also had an encyclopaedic knowledge of world culture and religions and they soon found they were before a judge who could make their prejudices wither on the vine.

He was reputed to have an adult son who was a doctor, a second son who was a pupil barrister, a daughter who was a trainee optician and another daughter who was apparently still at Oxford University studying atomic physics. His wife Fatima apparently kept an immaculate home and was a local magistrate.

District Judge Laura Stolinska was the youngest of the judges present. Her long blonde hair was loosely tied back. A large pair of dark ringed glasses made her look older than she really was. Only forty-one she had been appointed a District Judge at a relatively youthful age. Divorced, without children, when she was not working prodigiously hard, she gave her time over to hiking and cross-country running.

The judges sat round a large oval dining room table. There was a jug of water and some glasses in the middle of the table. The judges had an array of sandwich boxes and packets in front of them, but there was also a large plastic box of which Hassan Shah removed the lid and said,

"Fatima made us a few samosas. Please help yourselves."

Laura pushed a large paper bag into the middle of the table.

"I haven't brought anything for ages so brought these plums if anyone would like one. They might need a wash."

Bernard said to Nick, "Now and again one of us brings in some goodies to cheer up things."

Nick found he was being asked about himself and his family. Discussions then turned to news of things within the Combined Court.

"Utter disgrace that there is yet another delay in mending the leaks in the foyer," said Judge Shah KC. "And now the skylight over Court 2 has developed a leak as well. Good thing there has not been any rain today. The other week when I was trying to deliver a very sensitive judgement the sound of water pouring into buckets sounded as someone was taking a shower!"

Petunia said, "And I can see we are still the ''Ombined 'Ourt'…If any more letters drop off, we will just be a 'Binned out'!"

They all laughed at her joke.

"And what about the mice?" asked Bernard.

"I caught some scurrying across the ladies' floor," said Petunia.

"Well at least they were not on your desk," parried Bernard.

"Is that cat still about, Nick?" asked Petunia.

Nick said that he had followed him to the court today, but he did not know where he had gone. He explained about the stray turning up at the B&B and attaching himself to him and how he had been named Mr Perkins.

"Well, we could do with an army of cats being recruited rather than the £4000 desk in your room," said His Honour Judge Shah KC. "Sorry, Nick, nothing personal but it is not worth the money is it!"

Everyone laughed. There was then a "Miaow" and as if from nowhere Mr Perkins landed on the table with a thud. He sat bolt upright looking at all the judges.

"What a fine cat!" said His Honour Judge Shah KC. Mr Perkins purred like an engine.

Petunia said, "There is probably some rule that we shouldn't have him here, but I'm not complaining."

"Well, The Shadow won't like him," said Bernard talking of District Judge Roger Shadow.

"He doesn't like anyone," said Judge Shah KC. They all laughed except Nick who had yet to meet him.

Bernard looked at the clock, "Ten to two, back to work for me."

The judges packed up their food and went back to their courts and Chambers. Laura Stolinska found that Mr Perkins had decided to follow her back to her Chambers. As she opened the door of the tiny room which housed a kettle and her jacket and led to a toilet there was a rustling noise. Mr Perkins dived in ahead of her. Within a couple of minutes, he came out triumphantly with a dead mouse in his jaws.

"Why, thank you," said Laura, "I really hate mice. Sometimes they get into my larder at home, and I have to lay traps," she said of the old cottage in which she lived on her own.

He went to the door of her Chambers which she opened. He disappeared up the corridor still carrying his prey between his jaws. For a moment she thought how nice it would be to have a cat go into the larder and get rid of any mice which got inside. Just for a second, she also pictured a cat sitting by her hearth and welcoming her as she got home. Her thoughts then returned to her work.

While most of his colleagues had been sitting together in the judges' dining room District Judge Roger Shadow ate a lonely lunch of sandwiches from a small plastic box in his Chambers in the Circuit Court. He avoided the camaraderie of the judges' dining room at the Circuit Court. He did not like socialising. He did not like getting close to colleagues, he did not appear to like children or like animals; with a few exceptions he did not like anyone. It was his academic prowess and his detachment which had actually got him appointed as District Judge. He could muster up the polite formalities when he needed to do so, but otherwise there was something almost mysterious about him.

Colleagues and staff did not get to know about his home life. What few were aware was that when he was young his haughty demeanour had been shaken by an attractive fellow student with whom he tied the knot. His wife Sarah had given him twin daughters who had come into the world too soon, and so they had grown with difficulties in walking, talking and speech. Now aged nineteen they remained at home requiring round the clock care except when they went to a day centre three mornings a week. With no movement other than in their hands and lower arms and their necks and heads, their everyday needs had to be met by others. Sarah had worked tirelessly with them but about three years ago was diagnosed with a progressive condition herself, which was likely to affect her own future mobility. Roger's home was filled with a procession of carers or nurses. There was no room in his mind for friends or frivolity. He saved any warmth of feeling for Sarah and the twins. His parents were sadly deceased and although in the depths of his memories there were fond pictures of throwing a ball for their Springer spaniel they had as he grew up, he never discussed this.

Very tall, with black hair with white streaks and a large, hooked nose and angular cheekbones he did indeed have a sinister appearance. He sat alone eating the ham sandwiches he had made for himself. He read some legal articles and then picked up a newspaper. There was a small article about conservation projects and how woodland walks with friends and family dogs could benefit mental health. For a few seconds he mused about pleasant walks in the woods, but then dismissed the idea on the basis that he would of course be alone. He returned to reading about the law.

Meanwhile His Honour Judge Stanley D'Artagnon KC cursed the solitude of his lonely lunchtime in the spillover court behind the old Grammar School. A cheerful red-faced man his zest and zeal for different areas of the law was only matched by his enthusiasm for rich food, fine wines, brandy, and cigars. He had been married three times most recently to a young woman many years his junior. He had seven children of whom he was aware. He was also known for his enthusiasm for golf (especially the drinks in the clubhouse) and for attending every Circuit dinner which was ever held.

He would have preferred the company of colleagues to take his mind off some unwelcome news from his doctor. Routine blood tests and health checks had revealed high cholesterol and high blood pressure. His GP had lectured him that if he didn't improve his lifestyle the current lifestyle would soon kill him. He liked his cream trifle, his fried breakfast, his claret, his brandy collection, and his Cuban cigars more than he liked to admit; not to mention romantic trysts with the current Mrs D'Artagnon. He was worried that giving up or reducing his sins might not make him live longer anyway, but it would certainly feel like it. He too had found the article on the benefits of country walks but while he liked the idea, he wasn't sure his golf buddies would care for it. The current Mrs D'Artagnon, Cindy, only liked walking through shopping centres. His oldest children were at university, the middle children were sulky teenagers, and the youngest child was a fat crawling baby. He dismissed the idea and sat morosely chewing on a pork pie which he had brought with him. His late father Alec had left him with a taste for the finer things in life and it seemed hard to shake off that influence.

When Laura Stolinska returned to her Chambers to her pleasant surprise Mr Perkins was sitting just outside the door to it.

"Miaow," he said, looking at the door.

"Did you want go in?" she said bending down and stroking him.

"Miaow," he replied. She opened the door for him, and he went straight for the cloakroom area.

There was a brief scrabbling sound and he quickly reappeared with a mouse between his jaws.

"You are so good," she said as he disappeared up the corridor with his tail erect. "Tomorrow, I will bring you a reward."

Nick hardly noticed the lack of his feline friend as he had the return day of a Family Law Act injunction after having waded his way through mountains of family financial boxwork. The family injunction case was rather odd. The couple Akroyd and Harbelle Bosworth were very elderly. Each was supported by a family member who Nick later regretted allowing into the hearing, but in the light of their ages and lack of representation thought it was a good thing when he made the decision. Akroyd was supported by the couple's son Mark, and Harbelle was supported by their daughter Etta.

Apparently Akroyd was aged 85 and Harbelle was aged 83 and they shared the same house where they had not spoken for the last 30 years. Nick learned that now and again there would be a huge argument, and this was the sixth time there had been an injunction application or to be exact cross applications. The allegations by Akroyd were that Harbelle had smacked him on the backside with a rolling pin and that she had twice added washing up liquid to his coffee and that she called him a number of foul names. The allegations by Harbelle were that every time she walked past Akroyd he would jab her ankles with his walking stick and that he had fed the dinner which she had cooked him to the family dog. Each of them sought the other to leave the house. Nick was given to understand that past applications had also sought to oust the other party from the family home, but the applications were always settled by undertakings to the court, with each promising to behave.

Nick requested that he be able to discuss matters with the couple's children. He asked,

"Do you two get on?"

"Yes," they both replied.

"What about family occasions… how do you deal with those?"

Etta responded, "They still take place at Mum and Dad's house."

Nick ascertained that birthdays and other occasions were still celebrated in the normal way. He also found out that the couple were supported by a cleaning lady Monday, Wednesday and Friday mornings and that family members were frequently popping in and out of the house. There was a dog called Scruffy, acquired by Akroyd, and a cat called Flossy, acquired by Harbelle, who were doted upon by their non communicating humans. The couple did not speak except from time to time to insult each other about some trivial matter but from time to time they passed notes to each other, for example pointing out that there was a veterinary appointment. No-one had got to the bottom of the original quarrel 30 years ago. Previous District Judges had tried; all that anyone could ascertain was that things had gone downhill after their children had grown up.

Nick tried to probe this and found each of the couple had become quite weepy. He rang the bell for his usher to fetch a box of tissues for the couple. When she returned and left a box of tissues as asked, he thought that someone else had crept into the room. After a minute there was a thud and Mr Perkins jumped straight onto the desk and sat bolt upright in the middle of it looking disdainfully down on the snivelling old couple.

Harbelle stopped crying and said, "He looks just like old Tompkiss."

Akroyd stopped blowing his nose. "He does, doesn't he. Only difference was that Tompkiss had a little white patch on his chest... He's so handsome."

Mr Perkins purred. "You are a beautiful boy," said Harbelle enraptured.

The Bosworths both "oohed" and "aahed" about the cat and Nick thought he would take advantage of their united front about Mr Perkins.

"You both seem to like this cat here and clearly shared a love for a cat called Tompkiss, what happened?"

They both pointed at each other and spoke at the same time.

"She killed him."

"He killed him."

"Well, let's start at the beginning." Nick spoke soothingly. He managed to piece together the story.

It seemed that Tompkiss had reached the ripe age of nineteen and was a stiff and slow old cat. He never went further from home than the bottom of the garden but tended to lick up any spillages. Harbelle liked to scent the house with aromatic oils and Akroyd would frequently point out they could be poisonous to cats. Likewise, Harbelle would worry about Akroyd letting the cat in the garage in case he licked up anti-freeze. One day Tompkiss simply disappeared. There was a spilled bottle of lemon oil on a windowsill and some spillage of antifreeze in the garage with the door left open. It is true that the couple had had plenty of other niggles with each other which had become exacerbated when their children had recently flown the nest, but neither could explain where their beloved cat was. Each therefore blamed the other for the disappearance of Tompkiss and held that grudge for the coming years.

"Oh my God," said Mark and Etta in chorus, "it was us."

"What do you mean?" queried everyone else. Mark took the lead.

"One day I called round and Mum and Dad had gone to the shops or somewhere. I found Tompkiss on the doorstep. He couldn't stand. I picked him up and took him round to Etta's place. We both agreed that his back legs had gone, and he was fading away. We took him to the vets."

Etta nodded with a tear running down her cheek. "The vet said the kindest thing was to have him put to sleep, it was old age. He was nearly gone anyway."

Continued Mark, "Afterwards I had an autopsy just to be sure... then when Mum and Dad were at church, I buried him under the hedge at the bottom of the garden."

Etta spoke, "We debated about telling Mum and Dad. They were already grumpy about us having recently flown the nest, so we thought it might upset them too much if we said we had to have Tompkiss put to sleep."

"But surely you must have realised they had become so upset about something they were not speaking to each other?" queried Nick incredulous.

"Not for about a year. Because we became so busy with our own lives, and also Mum and Dad had often had phases of not talking much to each other," said Mark.

"Was the issue of Tompkiss never raised?" Nick queried.

"Not really, certainly they never said anything to us. I never thought the cat was the root of the issue," said Etta looking glum. "I think we did the wrong thing; I think we should have told them."

Soon everyone except Nick and Mr Perkins had tears running down their faces. Mr Perkins just purred.

Nick took legally binding promises from the Bosworths to not assault or harass each other but adjourned the case for 4 weeks.

"In that time, I want everyone to enquire about Family Therapy. I hope the whole family can engage in it. I would like to hear that you all have some commitment to attend such therapy or counselling so that I can dismiss the injunction applications. You all need to communicate with each other," he said.

Everyone piled out of Nick's Chambers except Mr Perkins who sat on the desk purring and looking smug.

Chapter 4

Mr Perkins seemed to have insinuated himself into "The Judges' Lodgings B & B" to the extent he now had a bed in a storeroom near the side-door and the old cat flap was put back into use. Having a cat bed between brooms and buckets was a cut above being left outside and did not impinge on the establishment's hygiene reputation since he was not allowed into the kitchens or food storage area. Somehow Mr Perkins seemed to know the limitations and Vicky Poletree marvelled at how he managed to keep himself away from any guests with cat allergies. Those who liked cats were regaled with loud purrs as he stretched himself across the reception desk. On weekdays he tended to follow Nick to the court but at weekends he spent his time around the B & B.

One Saturday Vicky managed to persuade him into a cat carrying case and take him to the vet for a check-up. Mr Perkins initially refused to come out of the box, and the vet had to take the lid off it. His expression was one of disgust as he was lifted onto the examination table by the vet who was a jovial middle-aged Welshman, Dylan Jones to whom Vicky had explained the situation.

"Well, you are a fine animal… and as a stray in amazingly good fettle, no fleas at all," said Dylan with a strong Welsh accent to Mr Perkins who now stood up and rubbed himself against him.

"Let's check for a microchip," said Dylan.

After he had done the check, he said to Vicky, "It's really strange. He has been chipped but I can't get a clear reading."

Vicky said, "I was hoping to find out whose cat he was… he's so friendly… with the loudest purr. That's why we call him Mr Perkins."

"I'll ask around," said Dylan, "but if you decide to keep him, you'll have to get him chipped."

Vicky nodded. "I had been thinking of adopting another animal… I think it would do Tasha good." She explained who Tasha was.

Dylan gave her a pile of leaflets from animal charities, "If you can't keep Mr Perkins these should give you food for thought."

Vicky said, "If he does not belong to anyone, I would be happy to keep him. I will not pass him to a rescue charity, but I will take the leaflets. If someone claims him, I might want another pet. I collect for Cats' Protection already. They do a terrific job for homeless and unwanted cats."

Dylan smiled and pushed back a mop of sandy brown hair which tended to flop forward.

"I am a volunteer vet at a couple of the charities… on my days off," he said. "Since I moved from Wales volunteering has been an invaluable way of meeting people."

Vicky wondered if he had any family at home and found her question was answered,

"It's just me and the gecko in my little house, you see," said Dylan. "My parents and brothers and sisters… and my ex are all in Wales."

Mr Perkins rubbed against him.

"Maybe you should get another pet of your own," said Vicky.

Dylan smiled as he lifted Mr Perkins back into his case and said, "Well. It's lovely to have met you and Mr Perkins."

When Vicky reached home, she opened the cat carrying case as soon as she was able and went to find Tasha. Tasha was in her studio at the top of the house, and to Vicky's surprise Mr Perkins followed her up the narrow stairs to an attic beyond the guest quarters. There were two large skylights which gave this room excellent natural light. Vicky worked in oils or pencil for her pictures and designs, but she was also a sculptor. There on a bench bathed in natural light was a breathtakingly accurate clay model of Mr Perkins. Although it was twice his size, it caught the enigmatic essence of the real animal.

Tasha did not hear Vicky and Mr Perkins enter the studio but felt the vibration as they reached the top step, so turned her head and smiled.

"How did things go?" Tasha asked. Vicky explained the situation.

"I do like having him round here," said Tasha. "Unlike the guests he doesn't shout at me or stare at my hearing aid or assume I am stupid."

"Well, you are far from stupid and in my opinion, you should be doing that college course on art, instead of just stopping here," said Vicky.

"I'm nervous of the other students," admitted Tasha. "I struggled with people at school."

"I know," said Vicky. "It was hard when you were little with glue ear and all the infections until you got a proper diagnosis."

Tasha nodded. "But children are so cruel... they mocked my hearing aid as I got older."

Vicky agreed and did not press the point. She went downstairs to reception to welcome her latest guests at the B & B. With it being clear she would have Nick Blyton staying for several months since his house transaction was going so slowly, and an influx of further guests who had made fairly lengthy bookings, business was good.

First to arrive was Herbie Greystock, a grey-haired whiskery gentleman of indeterminate age who had come to the area to find his ancestors. He had a small, round pair of glasses and a disconcerting looking mole next to one nostril. He appeared to be piled up with large cases. He had a slight North American accent.

"Not from round here, I can tell," said Vicky cheerfully.

"Not personally," he said. "But I kind of hope my ancestors lived in these parts. I am from Chicago, but since I retired from my optometrist business, I have been making it my business to build up a complete family tree. I have been to about a dozen places around the UK and my investigation brings me here… it's kind of my last hope. My partner Reuben has been pressing me to come home… he sure misses me."

Vicky wished him success and Mr Perkins appeared and rubbed himself around Mr Greystock's legs.

"Say what a friendly cat," said Mr Greystock. Vicky smiled and Mr Perkins had a glint in his yellow eyes, as if he harboured a secret. She showed Herbie to his room and told him when meals were available. When Vicky got downstairs Mr Perkins was still stretched across the desk, so she stroked him and said,

"I hope you stick around… you seem to cheer everyone up."

Mr Perkins didn't blink.

Cleo Callico needed cheering up. She had passed her foundation course in animal health, but there was simply no more money to carry on with her studies. Mum and dad could not afford to have her back home since dad was made redundant and now, she had fallen out with her boyfriend Fergal he had thrown her out after telling her that there were plenty more girls prettier than her! She had picked up her things off the front garden where he had thrown them and had stuffed them into her old knapsack which had come to rest on a thorn bush, and she had made her way to the bus station. She decided to spend her meagre resources on a ticket to the next big place, and a mobile phone enquiry to the "Judges' Lodgings B & B" had found her somewhere to stay for a few days. She sent a text to her mum to say she had gone to stay with a friend.

When she pushed open the front door of "The Judges' Lodgings B & B", she immediately spotted Mr Perkins and a smile lit up her face. She brushed aside her hair which was naturally blonde with a few dark streaks and pushed it back so that it did not dangle into her eyes.

"What a great cat," she said putting her battered blue knapsack down in front of the desk.

Mr Perkins purred and looked at her enigmatically.

Vicky asked her a few questions. Cleo looked clean and tidy due to a wash and brush-up at the bus station and her manner was polite. Vicky's instinct was correct that Cleo would be no trouble but was simply down on her luck.

"Do you want meals as well?"

Cleo shook her head and said, "I have enough in the bank to cover several nights in a single room, but I really can't afford a full English or a posh dinner each day." Then she added brightly, "I'm looking for work so maybe things will get better."

Vicky said, "Well there will be a complimentary cup of tea or coffee for you and a bowl of cereal in the dining room then at breakfast time… all part of the usual service."

It wasn't, but she felt sorry for Cleo who was quite young and appeared as if she had fallen on hard times.

Cleo smiled and thanked Vicky profusely. Vicky showed her to her room, with Mr Perkins following alongside.

As they went into the single room, which was the smallest in the establishment, Cleo said,

"Wow, this is lovely… are you sure it's for me?"

"Definitely," said Vicky. "I am glad you like it. Many solo travellers don't like it because it only has a single bed, and the telly is high up on the wall in order to fit in the desk, chair and wardrobe."

Cleo sat on the bed and Mr Perkins jumped up and she stroked him.

"Oh sorry," she said, "I don't suppose it's allowed. I just love animals and I hope I can find a job working with then. Although I'd settle for anything right now…"

Vicky smiled. "Well having animals on the bed is not generally allowed but I don't suppose Mr Perkins will take any notice of the rules. He is a stray, and we are trying to find his people but no luck to date. The vet couldn't read his chip…" her voice tailed off. "I wonder if Dylan the vet knows of any jobs…" she said thoughtfully, before leaving Cleo to unpack.

Mr Perkins stayed with her for a while and somehow, she felt less nervous for her future.

On Sunday Nick returned from spending time with his family. As he kissed and hugged them "goodbye" and patted Jasper the dog, he felt frustrated and melancholic by the delay to his house transaction. It was only when Mr Perkins appeared on his return that he felt slightly better.

Mr Perkins followed him down to the court on Monday morning. Renee Rollwright poked her head around the doorway to his Chambers as Mr Perkins sat purring on his desk.

"I'm sorry," he stammered looking at the cat, "he followed me in."

Renee smiled. "Well, I will pretend I didn't see him, as he has reduced the mice infestation, Judge. But I have actually come with some good news about our building. I am going to see all my judges because I thought you would like to know. Today, the lettering is being fixed and hopefully tomorrow will mean the start of some repairs to the leaks."

Nick said that he was very pleased to hear the news, and at lunchtime commented on it to His Honour Judge Shah KC and His Honour Judge Woldborough. They were the only three judges in the dining room although Mr Perkins put in an appearance. They were sceptical about the repairs to the sign and the leak. Bernard Woldborough stroked Mr Perkins and said,

"I think our puss-cat friend could do a better job. After all, he has the mice under control. It is as if he has taken charge." He paused and added, "A funny thing happened recently. I was hearing closing arguments in a particularly boring fraud case. I was worried a juror was nodding off and I didn't want to end up with discharging a jury member, or worse still a retrial. Suddenly, Mr Perkins, as everyone now calls him, jumps up out of nowhere with a thump on top of the desk in front of me... The juror shot up about a foot from his seat. Counsel paused and said, 'what is that, Your Honour?'. I just said, 'Pest control, please carry on'. Mr Perkins jumped down again and must have gone out of the courtroom. We just carried on as if nothing had happened and as if no-one fell asleep!"

Nick laughed and said, "Well I find him very therapeutic because as well as missing my family I miss Jasper, my dog."

Bernard Woldborough said, "I have a dog at home, a big mastiff called Beast, who is really a soppy dog. Likes his walks though! You'll have to come dog walking with me when Jasper arrives to your new house."

His Honour Judge Hassan Shah said, "My wife and I find our two cats very therapeutic. They are very beautiful, fine white Siamese cats with blue eyes. But this Mr Perkins is to my way of thinking a very intelligent cat."

"Miaow," replied Mr Perkins.

"He got into my court as well," he said. "The police had picked up a man I needed to deal with for breach of a family injunction and he was spinning me quite a yarn. All of a sudden, the cat appeared and jumped onto my clerk's desk. He stared the man in the face with those yellow eyes and then coughed up a large fur ball. The man stopped his whinging and excuses and said 'okay, I did it' and he was just pointing to where Mr Perkins had been sitting when the cat must have got down…. he just disappeared from my courtroom. No-one said anything, although I think there was a tiny mess on the floor. It was very strange in some ways."

He continued, "Anyway, I have brought him something."

He took from his pocket a snowy white linen handkerchief and a small plastic packet which said, "Dried sprat treats for cats". He laid out his handkerchief on the judicial dining table and emptied out four whole dried fishes onto it. Before he sat down to eat his meal, Mr Perkins purred loudly and rubbed himself against His Honour Judge Shah's hand. Not a scrap was left after the cat's meal. Soon the judges returned to their hearings and Mr Perkins padded off down the corridor.

When Nick was finishing his paperwork after his cases much later in the day, he was pleased to feel a rubbing around his legs and hear some loud purrs. Mr Perkins followed him outside as he headed back to the B & B. Nick paused to note that there was scaffolding outside the court, but the letters now read, "Combined Court". He assumed the scaffolding remained so that contractors might reach the leaks. A gust of wind blew, and a little piece of metal piping blew down off the scaffolding narrowly missing Nick.

Fred and Luke, the security men rushed outside when they heard the clatter, calling out "Are you alright, sir?"

Nick was shaken but uninjured but looked down to see Mr Perkins lying on his side next to the piping with his eyes closed.

"Oh no, oh no, oh no," said Nick.

The yellow eyes quickly opened, and Mr Perkins sat up plaintively holding up one paw.

"Thank God you're alive," he said to the cat.

"Mew," said Mr Perkins sadly.

"Is he okay?" said Fred.

"I think so," said Nick. Mr Perkins continued to hold up his paw and say, "Mew".

"But I'll get him checked out."

He gently picked up Mr Perkins and tucked him under one arm. Briefcase in the other hand "The Judges' Lodging B & B" seemed longer away than before, and the cat seemed surprisingly heavy. Vicky and Tasha were both behind the desk reception and Cleo was seated on a nearby chair looking at the job ads in the local paper. She had spent the day at an employment agency and peering at cards in shop windows.

"What has happened?" was the chorus as Nick gently put down Mr Perkins. Mr Perkins sat looking sad holding up his paw.

Nick explained about the scaffolding and said, "I'd like to get him checked out by a vet."

Vicky said, "I'll ring Dylan. He should answer because I know he does emergencies from what he said, but can you take him, as Tasha and I need to do dinner?"

"Yes of course," said Nick.

"I can help," piped in Cleo. "I like animals."

"I'll keep you some dinner," said Vicky after she had phoned Dylan and arranged the urgent appointment.

"I hope he is okay," said Tasha, "I wish I could come too."

Mr Perkins sat on a rug on Cleo's lap in Nick's car, rather than going in a carrying case. Nick had directions to Dylan Jones' surgery, and they pulled up right outside. Dylan opened the door.

"Sorry I'm on my own... a bit short staffed you know," he said.

Nick introduced Cleo and himself.

Dylan quickly took them to the consulting room where he examined Mr Perkins who by this time was standing up on the table and purring.

"I think he just had a bit of a fright," said Dylan, "I can't find anything wrong with him, so I think the paw holding was just him recalling an old injury."

Mr Perkins looked suitably enigmatic.

"Just keep an eye on him," said Dylan.

"We will," said Nick before enquiring about the charge.

"Forget it," said Dylan. "I haven't had to do anything... just put a donation into the tins for the animal rescue charities on your way out or 'Hearing dogs for the deaf'."

Nick asked if he could have some leaflets on the charities, particularly thinking of Tasha and the "Hearing dogs for the deaf". Dylan seemed happy to pile him up with leaflets. Then Cleo said,

"I know it's a bit of a cheek, but you said you were short staffed, and I have a foundation certificate in animal health. Do you have any vacancies?" she asked.

Dylan smiled. "Well, yes indeed. We are short on reception staff... We need an evening kennel maid come caretaker... Oh, and a clerical assistant."

"Please can you tell me how to apply for one of these?" asked Cleo. "I haven't got the paper certificate anymore but I'm sure my college can verify I passed the course, and my former tutor will hopefully give me a reference."

"My, you sound keen," said Dylan. "Come and see me the day after tomorrow, 2 o'clock sharp."

They smiled at each other, and Mr Perkins looked smug.

The cat sat quietly on Cleo's lap as they drove back to the B & B.

"He's fine," said Nick to Vicky and Tasha who immediately started stroking him.

"Other people are still on pudding, so you go and sit down and have your dinner," said Vicky to Nick.

"What about you, Cleo, are you hungry?" asked Vicky. Cleo looked embarrassed and was about to say "No," but Vicky said, "Spag bol and cheese board on the house for helping with Mr Perkins."

As for Mr Perkins he had stretched himself across the reception desk. There was something of a gleam in his yellow eyes.

Chapter 5

Next morning Nick looked up carefully before he entered the court. To his relief Mr Perkins had not followed him to the building and he concentrated on his family trial. He had left Mr Perkins sitting at reception with Tasha. She was working on the computer having finished her sculpture of Mr Perkins. The leaflet that Nick had given her on "Hearing dogs for the deaf" lay on the counter under a pot of pens. Her work on checking the future bookings was not going very well since Mr Perkins kept lying in front of the keyboard. After a while she attempted to lift him up, but he slightly scratched her. However, now he was at least standing up, albeit playing with the mouse. All of a sudden his paw also went on the keyboard and Tasha found herself reading from the website of the National Deaf Children's Society. It was a page about how to learn British Sign Language. Mr Perkins quietly jumped down as Tasha was intrigued to read from the website. She had thought about BSL before but had dismissed the idea since she had her hearing aid and could lip read. There was a reference to BSL being a great way to learn about deaf culture and community.

Tasha missed a small drama going on near the store cupboard. Vicky was talking to the regular cleaner and pot-washer Mrs Leana Grattwich.

"I'm so sorry to let you down," she said, "but Dad's eighty-eight now and the council carers don't stay five minutes… he's quite poorly and I think my last day will be Friday for my full hours. I can still do the pot wash and evening clean-up because I'll get my sister to sit with him then, but I can't do the rooms in the mornings. I'm so sorry but I have no choice."

Vicky glumly accepted the situation. She went to reception and told Tasha the bad news. Cleo was once again sitting nearby, studying the small ads, this time for flat shares and bedsits.

"Excuse me," she said, "I could help out. I don't know if anything will happen about the interview at the vets. I am desperate for work, any work. I will do a week's trial for free if it helps…? You have already been very good to me."

Mr Perkins said, "Miaow," signalling his approval.

"Why don't you give room cleaning a try on Saturday morning?" said Vicky smiling. "If it doesn't suit us, neither you nor I will have lost anything. I can show you the ropes then. If it is something we think might suit us both then I will pay you the going rate for say 2 hours per morning… with a bit of flexibility for both of us… Just give me a bit of notice if you find something better!"

Cleo was delighted at the chance. The potential for 14 hours work a week was better than no work.

"Miaow, miaow," said Mr Perkins. They all laughed.

Discussion turned to moving Tasha's sculpture to a discreet position on a windowsill near reception.

"You are really talented," said Cleo. "Are you at art college?"

Tasha shook her head and then retreated back to the computer. The page about sign language was displayed again. Mr Perkins rubbed against her legs. Somehow her curiosity had been piqued, and she found herself searching for beginner's classes in her area. She filled up an online enquiry form, hoping to pursue this further. When she looked down Mr Perkins had gone.

That afternoon District Judge Laura Stolinska was delighted to receive a visit from Mr Perkins in her Chambers. Whilst the mice had gone away at least for now, she gained a satisfaction from his presence. She stroked him and he purred like an engine and rubbed himself against her legs. As her list was over, she had just been checking messages on her mobile phone and had put it down in the middle of her desk. Mr Perkins jumped up and nearly went sliding off her desk again as his paw made contact with her screen.

"Whoa," said Laura, "what are you doing…?" as she picked up the phone before either cat or phone fell onto the floor.

The screen was now displaying an advert for the local cats' trust. Mr Perkins was sitting looking inscrutable. An endearing picture of a pair of tortoiseshell cats appeared on the phone screen.

"Good home wanted for Donna and Bella", was the heading. She went on reading,

"Mother and daughter need rehoming through no fault of their own. Approximately 6 and 2 years old. Would suit quiet household where there are no other pets and no small children since they are quite timid".

"Oh, Mr Perkins," said Laura, "you wouldn't be offended if I made enquiries for these ladies, would you?"

He looked enigmatic and purred. She sent a brief email to the cat rescue charity, and then went back to concluding her day's work by drafting a few orders on her Judicial laptop. When she had finished working, the cat followed her outside where she met Nick Blyton also leaving the building.

"Hello, Laura… hello, Mr Perkins," he said.

They looked up at the front of the building where the lettering was now looking splendid as "Combined Court" and was largely free of scaffolding. Just a little of it remained and some crawling boards for the roof repairs.

"Did you hear about his accident?" he queried. She nodded.

"He's okay... but I'm not sure this is the safest place for a cat. He's better off at the B & B where he seems very welcome," said Nick.

Laura mentioned she was thinking of adopting a cat or cats. Mr Perkins purred with approval. Laura went to the car park to fetch her car to drive home while Nick continued on foot as usual. Mr Perkins walked at the side of Nick as they strolled back to the B & B.

The following day while Nick was grappling with his difficult family case, it was also the day of Cleo's interview with Dylan Jones the vet. She had managed to contact her old college administration department who had emailed a copy of her certificate to her, and had told her that her old tutor agreed to provide her with a reference. Dylan asked her a great many questions which she did her best to answer. Then he said in a strong Welsh accent,

"Right, I'm not going to beat around the bush. This surgery as you can see is in a converted Edwardian house and we have a kennels and cattery on hand for some of our patients to stay pre and post op. I need someone in the building at night 8pm to 6am both so as to discourage the druggies breaking in and looking for drugs and also to keep an eye on the animals. Not that we have had any break-ins, mind, but it's better if a building looks occupied. I don't want to put you off. I need someone to check on the animals overnight and call me if something looks wrong… if an animal needed nursing obviously a veterinary nurse would stay. But otherwise, if they look okay, they would need checking on once or twice overnight. There's a little room with its own shower and toilet and I suppose I could arrange something, so you had a night off every week, some Bank holiday nights, and a holiday period 14 days a year… I can get another receptionist more easily… Is there any way you would be interested? I know it is not exactly the best job going."

Cleo said enthusiastically, "I am very interested. Can I see the room please? Would I be able to regard it as my permanent accommodation? It would be expensive and awkward for me to get a bedsit somewhere only to be sleeping here most nights."

Dylan showed her the room which was tiny compared to the room at the "Judges' Lodgings". It had nothing in it accept a single bed devoid of bedding and a small wooden chair. Ironically, the toilet and shower next to it was twice the size. Pay was discussed for her caretaking/animal duties. Cleo was calculating in her head her requirements and also considering whether she could also do the cleaning job for Vicky.

"Well, as long as you didn't bring in too much stuff, you could basically live here until you could afford something else," said Dylan. "There really is very little room."

Cleo concluded that if she had both jobs, although it might be tiring, she would be in a financially sound position, and might even be able to save up some money for a deposit on a little flat.

"When can I start?" she asked.

"I need to check out your reference," said Dylan, "but subject to that, as soon as it is practical for both of us."

They shook hands.

As Cleo walked back to the B & B she couldn't help wondering if Mr Perkins had brought her luck. It was something just short of a miracle that from being in danger of being on the streets, she now had prospects of not one, but two part-time jobs and a place to sleep.

However, Nick was not having a good day. He had a trial about contact and living arrangements for little Evangeline Karpack. If it was not bad enough for "Vanji" as her parents called her, to be saddled with a last name which sounded like "Car park" they seemed two of the most unreasonable litigants. Her father Constantine was a mechanic with a tendency to lose his temper, and her mother Marinda was a beautician who was apparently very argumentative. Arrangements between them were constantly breaking down, to such an extent Nick's predecessor had ordered an enquiry by Social Services under section 37 of the Children Act 1989.His predecessor had placed Vanji in the interim care of Social Services who had promptly placed her in the care of her maternal grandmother Marsophia. Marsophia had become a party to the proceedings and was content to look after Vanji and did her best to keep the parents from meeting each other, but yet still made sure there was contact to both. Marinda's parents did not hold any answers to sorting out the quarrels but were quite steady people. The grandmother and her husband were stalwarts of their local church, so Nick wondered if the argumentative Marinda's attitude was a reaction to her somewhat staid parents.

The Social Worker who went by the unremarkable name of Jane Smith recommended that Vanji should stay with Marsophia as she felt she could be trusted to give contact to both parents on a consistent basis (despite having no ability to stop the quarrels) and could in Vanji's best interests at least provide consistency and calm at home. However, despite months of wrangling she believed neither parent would obey court orders as to contact and would subject poor six-year-old Vanji to screaming rows at each handover which was in danger of damaging her mental health. The child had already developed a stammer after Constantine and Marinda had had a violent quarrel in front of her which involved them using wheely bins as battering rams against each other. The fight culminated with rubbish spilling out of a bin all over Vanji. Jane Smith said that the local authority had thus far tried mediation and negotiation and she also recommended that the parents engaged in some therapy; in order to assist the child and support the grandmother she recommended the local authority had a family assistance order for twelve months.

Nick had heard the evidence which included constant interruptions from each of the parents to each other's evidence and that of Jane Smith. He knew he was going to accept Jane Smith's recommendation since there were no other viable options, and, in the one-hour recess when he had gathered his thoughts in order to give an extemporary judgement, he had called on a security man to sit at the back of his Chambers. He was worried that neither parent would like his decision. As Fred entered his Chambers Mr Perkins sauntered in and sat himself on the side of his desk.

"Sir?" said Fred questioningly.

"Leave him," hissed Nick as the parties and Jane Smith sauntered into court.

As Nick began his judgement emphasising that he believed his decision was in the paramount interest of Vanji's welfare and addressing the welfare checklist under the Children Act 1989, he could see Constantine's face becoming increasingly thunderous. He was also aware of an odd clonk from somewhere behind and above him. High on the wall behind him was the

Royal Coat of Arms. He became aware out of the corner of his eye of a black cat swinging from it. He went on ignoring the dangling cat to explain his view of each party in as tactful language as he could, in particular emphasising the virtues of the grandmother.

"She's that bitch's mother. You moron," yelled Constantine.

"Be quiet." said Nick. "Any more remarks like that and you could find yourself in danger of imprisonment for contempt of court."

Instead of quietening down Constantine leaped up from his seat and made a massive jump over the gate onto the dais. He was just lunging at Nick when there was a "Miaow" and a hiss and Mr Perkins came tumbling down off the Royal crest landing fairly and squarely on Constantine's face, who then began teetering backwards.

"Ouch, aw, ow… ouch… I can't see," said Constantine wobbling towards the gate which was now being opened by Fred.

Fred stood back as Constantine seemed to fall back through the open aperture. He landed on the floor on his backside and Mr Perkins immediately climbed off him.

"Police, sir?" queried Fred.

"Are you going to behave now?" asked Nick to the litigant on the floor.

"Yes," said Constantine very quietly.

"Are you hurt?" queried Nick.

"No," said Constantine in a whisper. Mr Perkins seemed to have disappeared from Nick's Chambers, although Nick could not recall a door being opened.

"You may return to your seat, but Fred will sit next to you," said Nick.

"What was that, sir?" queried Constantine wiping a small trickle of blood from his face from a little scratch.

"What was what?" said Nick. "You tried to hit me and then fell over."

Constantine looked perplexed. Fred smiled wryly but looked straight in front of him. It had all happened in seconds so Marinda, Marsophia and Jane Smith were not sure what they had seen. They sat there quietly looking surprised and puzzled as Nick said to Constantine,

"If you behave yourself from now on there will be no need to call the police or to take contempt proceedings."

Indeed, he delivered the rest of his judgement with a silent Chambers and then everyone except Fred quietly filed out of the room.

Fred said, "Sir, should I say anything?"

Nick knew Fred meant, "anything about Mr Perkins". He replied,

"If you mean a report for your log or whatever you have to do about a litigant swinging at me and then falling over... just do what you need to do."

Fred nodded. He would not mention Mr Perkins.

When Nick came out of the building he looked up at the new lettering and was surprised to see it was wobbling. He was sure it was not supposed to do that, and he made a mental note to mention it in the morning. He was aware the buckets had been put to one side so that at least the leaks had been mended (for now).

When he returned to the "Judges' Lodgings B & B" he noted that Mr Perkins had arrived ahead of him and was stretched across the reception desk with a smug look on his face.

"You have reminded me of the importance of families getting on together," he said as he stroked him. "I'm going to phone my family at home and see if there is something nice, they want to do at the weekend."

Mr Perkins just blinked.

Laura Stolinska discovered she might have a new feline family by the weekend. She went to see Bella and Donna at the cat rescue that evening. They were in an outdoor enclosure with a shed attached as sleeping quarters. Although shy both cats allowed her to touch them. The cat charity manager arranged to drop into her cottage on Saturday afternoon, just to check on its suitability, although she said that she thought it was just a formality. Laura made a mental list of the things she would quickly buy, including comfy cat beds and bowls for food and water. Fortunately, the road was quiet outside her house, so if advised she could later put in a cat door giving her new companions access to outside. She hoped the visit really was just a formality as she couldn't wait to snuggle up on her settee with her new pussycat friends.

That evening in "The Judges' Lodgings B & B", Cleo phoned her mother for the first time for days.

"I'm so relieved to hear your voice… just getting texts is not the same. Where are you? Do you want to come home?" said her mum.

"I wouldn't dream of being a burden. You have the younger kids. But everything is going well where I am," said Cleo who explained a little more about where she was and her prospects for work.

"It sounds pretty good," said her mother, "but don't forget you still have a home if you really need it, and you can always come back for a visit."

"I will, Mum. Hopefully, you may be able to visit me for a day too once I am settled," she replied.

Mr Perkins rubbed against her leg and things felt very good for Cleo. She smiled and he rolled over for her to tickle his tummy.

Back at the court the lettering wobbled alarmingly in the breeze.

Chapter 6

Next morning Nick Blyton stopped in his tracks as he was approaching the court. There was a small crowd of people outside including a television outside broadcast crew. They were all looking up at the front of the building, in particular at the signage. More letters had dropped off and the sign on the building now read "Comb..ed C.u.t". Nick could not help a wry smile as he made for the rear entrance followed by Mr Perkins. The unfortunate situation with the letters was bound to end up on the local news.

It was at that lunchtime that he made the acquaintance of District Judge Roger Shadow and His Honour Judge Stanley D'Artagnon KC. District Judge Laura Stolinska was sitting elsewhere so she did not join them. His Honour Judge Hassan Shah KC was sitting in the old courtroom and had made his way across. District Judge Petunia Partington was in evidence as was His Honour Judge Bernard Woldborough. The judges were having a council of war about the state of the building hence Roger Shadow's presence.

Roger Shadow was glowering at everyone with an expression which if misunderstood would have been seen as pure malevolence. The reality was life was getting him down so much, and he did not know how to lift his spirits for the good of himself and his wife and the twins.

Stanley D'Artagnon introduced himself in jovial fashion and said with a laugh,

"Combed Cut! They'll think we are bloody hairdressers!"

Roger Shadow scowled, "Place is falling apart... if it hadn't been for some stray cat I hear has been hanging about, I believe we would be overrun with rodents. I think the roof is dripping again in the foyer."

Petunia agreed. "The heating and air conditioning don't work properly either... hot in the summer and cold in the winter."

Stanley D'Artagnon opened his lunchbox, and Bernard exclaimed,

"My God a salad! Whatever has come over you?"

"A desire to see my next birthday. My doctor has told me to live more healthily and to get more exercise," said Stanley looking a bit gloomy.

"You should get a dog," laughed Bernard. "Wendy, my wife, and I have a big soppy animal we call Beast. He gets us out on doggy walks."

Roger Shadow seemed to be listening intently. He looked less angry.

"Beast... stupid name," he muttered but kept listening.

"I miss my dog Jasper," said Nick who explained about the delayed house move. "These animals are very therapeutic. Somehow just walking with Jasper who has nothing to say but the odd 'woof' when he brings me his ball makes life seem better!"

Mr Perkins put in an appearance with a loud "miaow" as if announcing his presence.

"What's that?" said Roger crossly, glowering at the cat.

"This is Mr Perkins who got rid of the mice, the cat you mentioned," said Nick.

"He is a splendid animal," said His Honour Judge Hassan Shah KC.

"Who named him Mr Perkins?" asked Roger. "I thought he was some stray."

"He seemed to have named himself," said Nick. "It's the purrs you see."

Mr Perkins jumped up onto the table and sat right in front of Roger purring loudly and looking straight into his eyes. Roger seemed mesmerised.

"He's a little unnerving," said Roger after about thirty seconds. "Can't we give him a saucer of milk or something?"

"I thought you didn't like animals?" said Petunia.

"I never said anything like that," said Roger. "I just might have said in the past that I thought keeping pets was frivolous… but now…" His voice tailed off.

"Oh dear, I don't have anything today," said Hassan Shah KC looking in his pockets for animal treats.

"I might have half a packet of cat treats in my pocket," said Nick sheepishly and started rummaging. As well as a half-opened packet of cat treats the rest of the leaflets, he had gathered at the vets flew out of his pocket all over the table.

Stanley picked up a leaflet with a photograph of some dogs sitting appealingly. The heading was,

"Brothers seek homes".

There appeared to be three lurcher-alsation crosses sitting together. The charity said they were about six months old and housetrained but needed further training generally. They were described as children and animal friendly and had been living in a family foster home since their rescue.

"I might keep this," said Stanley, putting the leaflet in his pocket. No-one noticed Roger pocket an identical leaflet since Mr Perkins had started to chase an imaginary butterfly.

"Right," said Bernard, "what about the dreadful state of the building? Any thoughts as to what we can do without upsetting our hard-pressed manager?"

They decided that Bernard would email the Area Director and Stanley would email the Presiding Judge.

"Now," said Bernard, "shall we put the coffee on?"

Petunia helped clear Nick's leaflets away from the middle of the table and to Roger's colleagues' surprise he stayed with them for coffee. Petunia picked up a leaflet from the small collection. It extolled the virtue of pets for mental health support. She put it down again. Then she picked up another leaflet. Some pictures of rabbits and guinea pigs were on the leaflet which read "Busy Burrows Re-homing Centre. Rabbits and guinea pigs free to a good home". To her surprise the address was only a mile from her home. She put the leaflet into her pocket. Some part of her consciousness produced a mental picture of Milton stroking a small grey rabbit.

To their surprise Roger asked Bernard and Nick a few quiet questions about keeping a dog and then looked at his watch. "Back to Chambers," he said. "I have a telephone conference at 2pm sharp." He turned and left.

Nick was also surprised to find there were no leaflets left and less surprised to find that Mr Perkins was no longer in the room.

Tasha was sitting in reception again, that afternoon and was pleased when Mr Perkins jumped up next to her. She had received some positive information about local classes for British Sign Language. With much determination she filled out an online form to join the classes. The leaflet about "Hearing Dogs for the Deaf" still sat under the pot of pens. She stroked Mr Perkins.

Herbie Greystock was sitting in reception looking at his file of documents. He was speaking as much to himself as to Tasha,

"Well, I have looked in all the county records. I have looked at the historic index at the cathedral. I guess the only thing that is left is to trudge around graveyards."

Mr Perkins said, "Miaow," and jumped down to rub himself around Herbie.

Herbie was looking at a printed page which he had taken from his wall in Chicago. It must have been in a frame once and perhaps had come out of a book, but Herbie had just put a little adhesive tape on the back and stuck it on his cork board. It showed a picture of an old churchyard. Herbie then sighed.

"I wonder where this is?" he mused.

Mr Perkins stretched up to Herbie and suddenly the page came adrift and floated onto his back. It seemed to stick there. Herbie bent down to remove it and Mr Perkins went, "Miaow," and bolted for the door.

"Oh no," said Herbie and putting his file on the reception desk called out to Tasha, "mind my file please."

Although Tasha did not hear him, she understood what was going on and placed the file safely behind the desk.

Herbie dashed out of the front door following Mr Perkins who took him round to the hotel garden. He crossed the neat lawn of the garden. Mr Perkins leaped over the small wooden gate which led into the park. The paper continued to be stuck to him. Herbie opened the gate and continued in pursuit. Mr Perkins went across a small bridge over an ornamental pond and waterway, paper flapping and ducks quacking below. In retrospect Herbie often wondered why Mr Perkins did not move faster. It seemed just a fast walk by the cat, ahead of him and only just out of reach.

On the far side of the park Mr Perkins jumped over a low wall and the piece of paper which had stuck to his back flew off and landed at Herbie's feet. Herbie stopped in his tracks and picked it up. There in front of him was the churchyard in the picture. To one side there was a small chapel. By the gateway into the churchyard was a sign. Herbie read the sign,

"The Old Methodist Chapel Museum

Open Saturdays 12 noon to 4pm all year.

1 July to 31 August Fridays and Saturdays 12 noon to 5pm.

The Museum is dedicated to the Methodists in the area including,

Wesley Greystock who had this Chapel built".

Herbie smiled and some tears ran down his face. He folded the picture up carefully and put it in his pocket. He couldn't see Mr Perkins anywhere but if he had done so he would have hugged him! He began to look at the gravestones. Some of them were quite difficult to read. He tried the chapel door, but it was closed. He would come back when the museum was open, but here was clear evidence of his ancestors.

After he had been there for a good forty minutes, he became aware of a plaintive mewing sound. Mr Perkins emerged from behind a gravestone with first one and then a second bedraggled kitten. Each kitten was black like himself, but their coats were fluffy rather than smooth haired unlike Mr

Perkins and they had pronounced white whiskers. Herbie looked behind a gravestone and beheld a sorry sight. There was a larger black and grey cat evidently the mother cat lying stiff with her eyes closed. There was a trickle of dried blood by one ear and a stone next to her head. She was clearly deceased, and it was not clear if the presence of the stone was a coincidence or whether she had met a violent end. If there had been any more kittens they were no longer around.

The kittens mewed feebly at Herbie's feet, and Mr Perkins looked at him with a questioning gaze.

"I owe you one, buddy," said Herbie. "Do you want me to take the kittens?"

"Miaow," said Mr Perkins loudly rubbing against Herbie's legs.

First, Herbie covered the deceased cat with some leaves and made a mental note to contact the museum owner later. Then he gently picked up the kittens and cradled them in his arms. It brought back memories of his father's house in Indiana when he was a boy. Minister Ezra Greystock was a gentle soul who was kind not only to the farming folk who were his flock, but to any lame creature he found nearby. Sadly, Ezra had not lived to see the success of his son Herbie or to fulfil his ambition of finding details of his family tree.

He walked slowly back to "The Judges' Lodgings B & B" with the kittens in his arms and Mr Perkins by his side. As he crossed the bridge with the ducks quacking below the kittens "mewed" and Mr Perkins gave a reassuringly loud "miaow" in return.

By the time he arrived at "The Judges' Lodgings" Cleo and Vicky had joined Tasha in reception. Cleo had been discussing with Vicky her anticipated move to Dylan Jones' vet premises and how she would balance two jobs, when Tasha summonsed Vicky with concern about Mr Perkins and Herbie. Everyone looked at Mr Perkins and Herbie with much relief until they saw the bedraggled kittens.

Herbie sat down and told Vicky, Tasha and Cleo what had happened.

Vicky said, "I think you need a strong coffee. I'll put the kettle on..."

She came back quite quickly.

"It's another emergency call to Dylan, I think," she added.

She rang him and as before he was very helpful.

"Can you girls walk up there if I give you a basket and an old towel?" she queried as she rummaged and produced a wicker basket from a cupboard.

"Can I help?" said Herbie.

"No, it's fine, but thank you for asking," responded Cleo. "I'm going to work there shortly as a kind of night caretaker come kennel maid."

"Do let me know if they are okay," said Herbie looking concerned.

"Poor little things," said Tasha. "Maybe we can keep them."

Vicky just raised her eyebrows. Mr Perkins said, "Miaow," and settled himself on the counter as the girls started walking.

Dylan gave the bedraggled kittens a thorough examination. Cleo and Tasha told him the story. He smiled at the girls and said,

"What is it about the B & B and that Mr Perkins? Suddenly we have frequent visits! And I'm even getting my new employee!"

The girls laughed.

Tasha asked, "Are they going to be okay? I'd like to keep them if possible."

"Well," said Dylan, "these poor little things are just about weaned. They will need their injections and they will need chipping. If you don't want more kittens, they will need spaying in a few months' time. Are you up for all that? If not, I think we should contact Cats' Protection."

Tasha replied, "I would like pets of my own," who had lip-read all he had said.

Dylan asked, "What about the hearing dogs? I gave that guy a leaflet when he brought in Mr Perkins with Cleo. It is a great organisation."

Tasha said, "I haven't really read things yet, but I do want these kittens."

"What are you going to call them?" said Dylan.

Tasha replied, "They are very lucky to be alive. I have been reading old myths and legends, so I reckon that they deserve some Norse or Greek goddess names, but I don't know enough about the stories."

"I like the old Celtic and Norse stories," said Dylan. "It's a bit of a hobby of mine. How about Frigg... the goddess of foresight and Sif... the goddess of earth and homes. It kind of fits!"

Cleo said,

"They had the foresight to be found by Mr Perkins so now they are going to get a good home, I am sure!"

Tasha and Cleo agreed that the names fitted and arranged a series of appointments to have the kittens inoculated against cat flu and other diseases and also to have them chipped and then took the kittens home to "The Judges' Lodgings B & B". Dylan gave them plenty of advice about how to provide for the kittens in the immediate future.

When they arrived back Vicky and Mr Perkins were manning the reception desk and Herbie was sitting nearby.

"Are they OK?" said Herbie. "I just rang my partner Reuben Mandelstein and told him the story... how Mr Perkins led me to the graveyard... how he found the kittens. Reuben is real pleased I will be home soon, but he says he is going to fly over for a week or so, so that he can be with me when I finish my research. I am going to try and persuade him that we should get a cat when we return to Chicago!"

Everyone smiled and wished him luck with getting a cat.

Nick arrived as everyone was talking and immediately saw the kittens. He was told the story of how Mr Perkins found them.

"So that's what he did this afternoon," he laughed.

Tasha said, "I'm going to keep these kitties in my studio for now, although I need to go and get some things for them, litter tray, bed, kitten food..."

Nick said to Vicky, "As long as you keep some dinner for me, I'm happy to go for her."

And Herbie added, "And if you don't mind me tagging along, I would be pleased to pay for the items as a gift for helping me find my forebears!"

Nick and Herbie went off to the pet supermarket in Nick's car, while Tasha and Cleo took the kittens up to the studio. Mr Perkins sat on the reception desk looking smug.

Petunia Partington on the other hand looked nervous when she got home. First, she had to ask husband Joe about the prospect of keeping a rabbit or rabbits and then it was a question of whether Milton would be receptive to the idea.

Joe, ever practical said, "It's worth a shot. As long as he doesn't dissect some poor animal it might be up his street to have a pet."

Milton was fiddling with his bicycle outside when Petunia said, "Milton. Would you like to visit the rabbit rescue on Saturday with a view to having a pet rabbit?"

A broad smile lit up his usually worried looking face, "You mean I could have a pet rabbit all of my own... to be my friend?" he asked.

"Absolutely," said Petunia. "As long as you looked after him or her... I'm not particularly used to pets so you would need to do a lot of the work."

This was true. Petunia's family had not had pets, so she had simply never considered having a pet in the household until now. She knew Joe had had pets when he was young living with his parents, but he had never pressed the issue with her. She was sure he would keep an eye on Milton and his rabbit.

Milton said brightly, "Do you think we ought to look on the computer and see what we might need?"

"Good idea," said his mother, delighted to see the enthusiasm. "But make sure you finish your homework first."

"Oh, Mum," he replied rolling his eyes behind his spectacles. "I finished it ages ago... it was boring and easy. It was all about small mammals and their habits... Funny though. It sounds like I'm getting one."

Petunia laughed with him and added, "Well homework is important if you want to do anything worthwhile when you grow up."

"Of course, I know that," said Milton. "I want to be a vet or a zoologist. I did think about being a fireman, but I have grown out of that idea."

This was the longest conversation Petunia had had with Milton for weeks. She smiled and said,

"Have I told you about the cat which has been visiting the court?"

"No," said Milton. "You never tell me anything about the court."

It was true she never really mentioned work to him. As best she could Petunia told Milton about Mr Perkins and what she knew of his activities at the court.

"He sounds a very clever cat," said Milton. "Maybe one day we could have a cat like that one too?"

"Well," said Petunia, "let's start with a rabbit!"

Chapter 7

There was scaffolding at the front of the court again as staff and judges left work for the weekend. Roger sighed as a rodent scuttled across the car park. At least that cat had kept the mice under control indoors. He had experienced an awkward afternoon. In a care case with which he was dealing, the child, a thirteen-year-old girl, had asked to see him. He had taken advice from the children's guardian, and it had been agreed that the guardian, and the social worker would be present. She would be told the encounter would be recorded but the rest of the people in the case would not attend.

His Chambers for the afternoon were arranged a little more informally and tea and biscuits was to be offered. He scowled at everyone else at court that day until the meeting with thirteen-year-old Sincerity. Then he managed to compose his face to one which was just serious. Sincerity seemed very nervous and had to be prompted by the social worker to speak. Suddenly from nowhere Mr Perkins appeared and jumped up on the table nearest Sincerity.

Roger said sternly, "This is a stray who has appointed himself court rodent officer, but I can have him removed if you don't want him in here."

"He's lovely," said Sincerity. "He can stay." She started stroking him and he purred loudly.

"You like animals?" said Roger using the opportunity to bring her out of her shell.

"Yes," she said. "That's why I want to live with Auntie if I can't go home. She has a farm with loads of animals."

Sincerity's mother was in prison for supplying cocaine and her father was an Albanian who no-one could find, and she was currently living with her grandmother. The social worker favoured Sincerity living with her granny in the same area as she had lived with her mum, but Sincerity did not seem happy about this. A half-sister of her mother had been located about 70 miles away, who was of farming stock and who was pleased to get to know Sincerity recently and now offered her a home.

"What about changing school or seeing your granny?" asked Roger.

"I don't mind about school, I only have a few friends there and we can keep in touch on social media. A lot of them are just into fashion and they make fun of me reading about nature and stuff. Granny means to be kind, but I think she finds me a bit much... she'd prefer to play bingo and I know she wants to go to Spain without me for a holiday with her new boyfriend Glenn... Tea with her once a month would be fine." She stroked Mr Perkins, "Auntie Stacey says I can have a pet of my own to make me feel better... She has horses, chickens, ducks, all sorts at the farm."

Roger could not help but feel a pang of sadness. She was a lovely young girl and didn't deserve her situation any more than the twins deserved their situation.

Sincerity said suddenly, "Does the cat make you feel better too?"

Roger was startled and mumbled, "I think he does." He thought the child was very intuitive to notice that he needed to feel better.

Mr Perkins looked enigmatic, and after a few formalities the meeting came to an end. As Sincerity left, she said, "I do like the cat. He made things much easier." Without thinking about it, Roger quickly stroked Mr Perkins before he left the building for the car park and was rewarded by a purr like an engine. Mr Perkins went outside too and then disappeared into the shadows between the buildings.

When Roger reached home, his wife Sarah was all smiles.

"I have had an excellent review with my consultant today," she said. "He said my medication is working so well that I have not had any further decline in mobility at all over the last 12 months. Hopefully, my condition is now stable and won't decline for a long, long time."

Roger expressed his pleasure in the news, and she went on,

"He did express surprise that I did not go out more and suggested I should get out and about and that I should have a mobility scooter in case I should get tired…"

"What about the twins?" queried Roger.

"Well," said Sarah, "when they are at the day centre or with carers, I can't see why I should not say get some fresh air… in fact if I got a folding scooter, we might go to places together like we did years ago. You might take the odd day off so we could do something nice; it would do you good as well."

"Maybe," said Roger, and Sarah continued,

"He said it would benefit my health if I got out for things other than medical appointments for myself and the twins. As for having a mobility scooter I can't think why I didn't get one years ago."

"I suppose we should consider it," said Roger cautiously. He was so used to seeing Sarah always at home unless she or the twins had medical appointments.

He went to see the twins who were sitting in wheelchairs in a conservatory he had added to the house.

"Hello, Cassie… Hello, Diana," he said and also "signed" "Hello". The twins used British Sign Language as their hearing and vocalisation was impaired. He knew a little of "Signing" which he used as much as possible. It was difficult for him to keep up with the twins in signing as his use of the language was limited to the time he spent with them. However, he could see the benefit to them of BSL. The girls seemed in a good mood and as far as he could understand had enjoyed their time today at the day centre, in particular socialising with other young people.

Roger did his best to explain about the clever cat at the court and how he was known as Mr Perkins. Cassie asked him if one day they might have a cat or a dog as a pet. He was surprised by the request. She had never asked before but then he had never told them about a clever cat before. Sarah joined them.

"The girls are asking if perhaps we might get a pet. What do you think?" he asked Sarah.

"You have taken me by surprise," she said. "I had never thought about it. I suppose having say a dog would get you out and about for walks. Sometimes I could join you on the mobility scooter which I would like to get…"

"Whoa, everyone," said Roger, nevertheless smiling for once, "let's take a step back. We should do some research before jumping into things."

Sarah took a handful of papers off a nearby table which were printouts of mobility scooters. Without thinking Roger took the leaflet about the young dogs needing homes from his pocket.

"I think we have some reading to do," he said. "I won't make promises. In respect of the scooter, I want to make sure you have the best on the market for your needs. As for a dog I think I should take advice about what it should entail for us… and maybe… just maybe look at one of these dogs."

In his mind's eye he could see himself walking in open fields throwing a stick for a doggy companion. He could also see himself walking along the paths in the park, dog on lead and Sarah beside him. He could also see a friendly dog who would sit by the twins and let them touch him and stroke him. He hoped it was not all a pipe dream. Somehow in his consciousness the enigmatic look of a cat invaded his thoughts. When he went to bed that night his dreams were full of dog walks and picnics in the park with Sarah, the twins and a doggy companion. As he surfaced his dream became more peculiar. Mr Perkins was sitting in his judge's chair at court complete with a wig and he was standing in the dock holding the dog rehoming leaflet. A couple of 'miaows' came from Mr Perkins' mouth which sounded like 'Do it, do it'.

He woke with a start. Sarah said, "Are you alright, dear? You were talking in your sleep and said, 'I will do it'." He muttered that he had been dreaming and decided to spend the rest of the weekend researching mobility scooters and what he would need to keep a dog.

When Petunia Partington got home for the weekend at first there was nobody to be seen.

"Joe? Milton? Where are you?" she called out. There was no answer in the house.

She went outside and called again when Joe appeared from the bottom of the garden looking harassed,

"Little blighter has climbed up a tree and won't come down…" he said. "I'm going to get a ladder."

Petunia went to the end of the garden and looked up into the big old horse-chestnut tree where she saw Milton sitting on a branch.

"Why are you up there?" she asked.

"There's a pigeon's nest in the tree," he said. "But I saw a hawk swoop down and I wanted to check the little birds were okay."

"Are they?" asked Petunia.

"I think so," said Milton.

"Well, it would be better you got down… or the mother pigeon might not come back," responded Petunia.

"I am stuck," said Milton. "I tried to tell Dad."

At that moment Joe appeared with a ladder which he leant against the tree.

"Can you reach the ladder on your own if I hold it steady for you?" asked Joe.

"I think so, Dad," said Milton who edged along the branch he had been sitting upon, and then scrambled down the ladder.

Joe said as he removed the ladder, "You must never ever do something like that again, you could have fallen and been badly injured."

"Sorry," said Milton in a miserable voice looking at the ground.

Petunia added, "I thought you had learned your lesson with the Primary School roof." They started to walk back to the house.

Milton looked as if he was choking back tears.

"I really am sorry... animals and birds are my friends... I like to help them," he said.

"Still not going well at school?" queried Joe.

"I got an A in a test about identifying mammals, but the other children were cross 'cos I beat them again and called me names in the playground like 'nerdy pants', 'four eyed git' and 'teacher's favourite'." A tear ran down Milton's face. He adjusted his spectacles and wiped his eye.

Petunia said, "I will speak to your teacher again. But how would you like a pet?"

Milton started to smile, and Joe looked perplexed.

"A pet?" said Joe. "Who on earth is going to look after whatever... I shan't... I thought we agreed no animals until he learned to behave."

Petunia showed Joe the Busy Burrows leaflet.

"I thought if Milton had something of his own, it might teach him to be responsible. He will have to clean it out and make sure its needs are catered for..."

Joe looked thoughtful, "Well if he'll stop climbing things."

"Please, please, Dad. A rabbit to be a friend of my own would be so good. I would keep it clean and not climb things," said Milton imploringly.

"Well, maybe," said Joe. "Although I wish you could make some friends in your class at school."

Next morning the Partington family made a trip to Busy Burrows. They debated about simply cycling or walking there as it was only a mile from home but in the end decided to take the car since they hoped they might need to transport a rabbit and his equipment. Milton was enthusiastic about all the rabbit and guinea pig residents and was full of questions to the owners Tessie and Michael Humberstone and their volunteers.

"Well, you are keen," said Tessie to Milton. "If your mum and dad will let you, you'll have to join our volunteers cleaning out the animals and caring for them."

"Can I? Can I? Can I?" asked Milton. Before they knew it Petunia and Joe had agreed to Milton spending his Sunday mornings with the volunteers.

"And what about a rabbit to live at our house?" asked Milton.

They looked at all the animals who were wanting homes. There was a huge Belgian hare who went by the name of Benji who enthralled Milton, but Petunia was concerned over his size. Eventually they reached the end of a row of hutches and at the very end was a hutch containing a small grey lop-eared rabbit and a large white and ginger guinea pig. On a piece of cardboard taped to the hutch were the words "Katy rabbit and Billy guineapig, best pals". They sat side by side apparently sharing a carrot. Milton looked entranced.

Tessie was nearby collecting a small hay bale from a shelf and saw their interest.

"They are best pals. Apparently, their former owner got Katy first but then acquired Billy as company for her, but sadly the family had to move to a place which didn't allow pets. We think they are both about a year old and we will only let them go on the basis they are kept together," she said.

"Mum? Dad? Please...," said Milton.

Joe looked at Petunia who nodded slightly and said, "Well we can't take them immediately because we need to buy a hutch, food, and other equipment, but if Mum says, 'yes', maybe we can reserve them and come back later this afternoon."

Petunia said, "Yes, of course," and asked Tessie what donation was required for the rescue centre to secure the arrangement.

"Well," said Tessie mentioning a figure. "We have to cover the cost for the time they spent with us, but I will do a deal. Milton seems very keen to be here. On the basis Milton turns up for at least the next four Sundays as a volunteer I will reduce the amount by a half."

Milton said, "I would really like to help on Sundays. Other boys do football and stuff, but this could be my thing... something for the animals."

Joe and Petunia thanked her and obtained a list of items to buy from the local pet supermarket. Milton beamed as they drove off to buy what was necessary. He beamed even more when they returned to collect Katy and Billy. They were placed in a cardboard animal carrying case which sat next to Milton on the short ride home. Joe and Petunia were impressed how organised Milton seemed in setting up the hutch on the patio, under an awning near the back door. He then sat down at the kitchen table with his computer tablet and came up with a chart for a programme of feeding his new friends and cleaning the hutch. After that he went outside with a carrot to check his new friends were alright. As they nibbled Milton said thoughtfully,

"Everything is going to work out for us."

Back at "The Judges' Lodging B & B" Herbie Greystock was sitting outside on a bench talking to Mr Perkins in between making some notes on a tablet about his ancestry searches. Mr Perkins had placed his two front paws on Herbie's left leg and was purring like a motor. Herbie found that if he stopped stroking his feline companion Mr Perkins stuck his paws into his leg, so he was finding it hard to make his notes.

"Are you trying to tell me something?" said Herbie.

"Miaow," came the response. Herbie laughed but then he heard the sound of a car draw into the driveway. He looked up and saw it was a taxi. To his pleasure and surprise the man alighting from the taxi was none other than Reuben Mandelstein. Reuben paid the driver and then stood for a few seconds with his bags as the taxi departed. He opened his arms wide and gave Herbie a big bear hug.

"Miaow," said Mr Perkins in a knowing way and followed them indoors.

"He knew you were coming," said Herbie.

Reuben bent down and stroked him. "You are the clever one who found Herbie's people."

"Miaow," responded Mr Perkins.

Vicky greeted Reuben affably and asked Herbie if she should bring more towels to his room and whether anything else was required. Reuben was a large, whiskery man a bit like Herbie in appearance.

"I'm real tired," said Reuben. "I have been on a train to O'Hare Airport, then on a plane, then 2 different trains and finally a taxi. I want a hot bath and a long sleep."

"Miaow," said Mr Perkins as if in agreement. Reuben laughed.

"Is that cat trying to demonstrate how clever he is?" he quipped.

Vicky smiled and said, "No demonstration is really necessary. He seems to have a remarkable effect on people."

Reuben smiled. "You know when I had my dental practice one of my nurses maintained that pets really calmed people. She had a family of Siamese cats, but I couldn't let her bring them in... However, we got a fish-tank and I really think it helped people to look at the fish if they were nervous. When I retired, I gave it to the guy who took on the practice... My Aunt Irmgard who brought me up had two cats she kept in her apartment, Georgie and Pippi. We even took them on little vacations to a cabin on the shores of Lake Michigan. They had died before she went to a home for seniors and before she died herself."

"You never told me this before," said Herbie.

Vicky laughed and Mr Perkins looked enigmatic.

"Well, I guess we can talk more about cats when I have had some sleep," said Reuben.

They went upstairs. Vicky went to fetch some more towels. Then she went to see Tasha and Frigg and Sif the kittens. They had some string and were chasing a long piece of it energetically. She managed to get side-tracked for a good twenty minutes before she returned to reception. She looked around for Mr Perkins, but he wasn't in reception anymore. She formed the conclusion he would turn up again when he was hungry or indeed if someone needed him.

Chapter 8

Cleo Callico smiled as she considered her little room at the veterinary practice. It was not much but thanks to Mr Perkins she had a job and a little place to call home. She resolved that she would continue to help out at "The Judges' Lodgings B & B" as long as she could manage it as well. She felt she owed it to Vicky and Tasha who she regarded as her friends. It didn't bother her that she was the only person in the veterinary centre overnight.

She found herself sitting in the room with the overnight "guests" making reassuring noises to the cats and dogs who were unfortunate enough to need medical treatment. Subject to any instruction she had received she opened the odd cage and stroked some of them.

With Cleo now installed at the surgery Dylan Jones now found the time to consider his own needs. His surgery was one of the few in the area not part of some huge chain. He employed three vets, two full-time and one part-time. He was contemplating making at least one of them partners. He had bought a little house not 10 minutes away from the surgery. It felt a bit empty now he thought about it. Just him and a gecko.

Since it was the weekend and he was not running a clinic, he went out for a stroll and soon found himself at the B & B. He was greeted by Vicky and Mr Perkins.

"Miaow," said Mr Perkins.

"Hello," said Vicky who had had her head in an accounts' ledger. "Can I help you?"

"It's me. Dylan the vet," he said. "I just thought I would pop in since I was passing."

"Of course it is," said Vicky. "It's Tasha you saw with animals most recently. I was distracted. Would you like a coffee?"

Dylan accepted and sat talking partly to Mr Perkins and partly to Vicky.

"It really is a nice place here," said Dylan. "No wonder Mr Perkins moved himself in. It's a good position near the park. When I get a dog of my own again, I can see me calling by for coffee, unless that causes a problem about bringing a dog here?"

Vicky smiled. "A vet without a dog of his own? Who would have thought it?"

Dylan explained about how busy he had been with his practice and that after his dog had died some years ago and his marital split, he had not got round to getting another dog of his own, although he had his gecko, Graham.

Vicky answered his question about calling in with a dog. "I guess the garden is no problem as long as your doggy doesn't leave his doings everywhere!"

"Well, I will have to call in again soon!" said Dylan.

"Miaow, miaow," said Mr Perkins.

"Did you ever find Mr Perkins' people?" asked Dylan.

"Still looking," said Vicky. "I will have to get him chipped soon and officially adopt him if I still can't find his people."

"Well, we can't have you breaking the law!" joked Dylan.

When Dylan got home, he started looking at a leaflet which said, "Brothers need homes". He resolved he would make plans to adopt one of these brothers or another needy mutt. He and his ex-wife had never had any children and he had devoted so much time to other peoples' creatures he had omitted to get his own pet apart from the gecko in recent years.

Stanley D'Artagnon KC was not having a good Saturday. The latest Mrs D'Artagnon was berating him for not doing any gardening, decorating or anything useful around the house. Smallest D'Artagnon was showing signs of walking and was taking a distinct interest in his wine rack. The bottles wobbled alarmingly as he tottered round that part of the room.

"You need to sort things out and make the rooms safer for Cliffy," she said.

"Cliffy? Cliffy?" he queried. "His name is Clifford… Cliffy makes him sound like a dog." His voice tailed off as he returned to the idea of having a dog. He pulled the leaflet about the brothers needing homes from his pocket.

"Right," he said, "we are going to make some changes round here. First, I am removing your make-up table from the dining room, and I am taking it upstairs to our bedroom since we have plenty of room in the master bedroom. Then I will remove the wine rack from the small sitting room and place it in the dining room. Then I am buying a dog bed and putting it there instead… Then I am blocking up holes in the hedging in the back garden to make it safe for Clifford and a dog. Then, we are getting a dog!"

Mrs D'Artagnon sat with her mouth open and after few minutes said,

"I don't want an animal to harm Cliffy... I mean Clifford."

"First," said Stanley, "I won't choose one with a bad track record. Second the dog will need to be trained. I will take part in the training. I think it will not only improve my health to be out dog walking, but it will be good for our child to grow up with a pet."

He showed his wife the leaflet.

"I suppose so," she said grudgingly. He got to work with the tasks he had given himself. To his pleasant surprise he enjoyed pottering about the garden. While he would retain the services of his gardener, he realised he had been missing out by not spending time in the garden. Soon his wife and Clifford came outside as well. She held the child by the hand as he made teetering steps around the grass.

Stanley said, "I am making a list of things we need for the garden like a bit more fencing and maybe some decent garden furniture. I think I will get a little swing for Clifford and put that up in the garden too."

Most of his progeny didn't bother with him except if they wanted money. There was an expectation that he could magic up resources. He had of course been to public school and Oxford University and had had a glittering and remunerative career at the Bar. Indeed, he had only taken judicial office to ensure he had regular rather than sporadic income. The large semi on a pleasant but decidedly ordinary housing estate was not a place where many would expect a top silk or indeed a top judge to live. The truth was he had a hard time balancing the books, not assisted by his tendency for over-indulgence. He had no family money behind him. Not even his own children were aware that he narrowly missed being called Stanley Drain. His late father Arthur Drain had been a petty crook and door to door salesman. After twelve months inside for breaking into a warehouse he came out and decided to turn over a new leaf and adopt a new identity. He changed his name to Alec D'Artagnon as he thought it had a cultured ring and he then fell on his feet as a car salesman. When he changed his name, he also got his pregnant wife Doreen to change her name to Daphne D'Artagnon. By the time Stanley was three years old, Alec had a flourishing chain of car showrooms and Stanley could be sent to the best schools. Daphne was still alive now but lived in comfort in a retirement home funded by the proceeds of sale from the car showrooms, although she barely recalled who anyone was.

For a second, Stanley thought he saw the face of a cat staring at him from under a hedge. The yellow eyes looked so like those of Mr Perkins. Then the animal was gone. He continued his gardening.

Tasha had recently enjoyed socialising with the other youngsters in her British Sign Language class and she greatly enjoyed playing with her kittens who she was sketching. Being part of the deaf community was broadening her horizons, but she still spent a lot of time on her own in her studio where she happened to be on Sunday afternoon.

There was a thump on her table and a feline mouth said, "Miaow," and this did not emanate from a kitten. It was of course Mr Perkins who jumped up on the table. He stood on her art materials and was very insistent. She stroked him but he was not to be moved and she felt the vibration of his purr. When she lifted him down there on the table she spotted "Hearing dogs for the Deaf". He rubbed against her legs and when she tried to get on with her art she felt his claws in her leg.

"Ouch," she said. "Why did you do that?" He jumped up again and knocked the leaflet on "Hearing dogs" into her lap.

"Alright, alright," laughed Tasha, "I will look at it." Mr Perkins purred and looked smug.

A paw rested on her leg. "Really I will," she added. He quietly left the room as she began reading the leaflet and then she went online to read some more. She was encouraged that the concept of assistance dogs was recognised by the NHS and that they were trained not to bark to attract attention, but to alert their person by touch. There was particular emphasis on helping with confidence and combating loneliness. While Tasha would not have said she was lonely she knew her lack of confidence held her back. She resolved that on Monday morning she would start making tentative enquiries to her most local assistance dog centre.

That Sunday afternoon Nick brought his wife Danya, daughter Maria, son Harry and dog Jasper to the "Judges' Lodgings B & B". As well as his usual room Vicky had made a second room available to the family. After all these weeks, finally, he was near to completing his house purchase and since the children were on school holidays he brought them to explore the area. There was a cacophony of noise as they descended from his vehicle. As they entered reception Jasper started barking at Mr Perkins. The cat looked disdainfully down from the reception desk and slapped their red setter Jasper smartly on the nose with an outstretched paw.

"Ger, waw, waw," went Jasper and sat down behind his master.

"I think we know who is in charge," said Danya.

"What a fine pussy," she continued and stroked Mr Perkins who purred.

The family made suitably admiring comments to Mr Perkins and then went to their rooms to unpack.

On Monday morning Nick decided to give Danya and Maria a tour of the court, while Harry looked after Jasper. Although on annual leave he thought it fitting to show family members where he worked. Of course, Mr Perkins followed them to the court.

Danya said, "Isn't there something wrong with the lettering?"

"Not again," said Nick looking at the letters which read "Com.in…ou.t".

"Come in out," giggled Maria.

"Miaow," said Mr Perkins, so Nick told his wife and daughter about the incident with the cat outside the court, but how fortunately he was not hurt. Then they went into the court and Nick gave them a tour. Mr Perkins followed them inside causing Maria to smile and say, "I really hope we get a kitty as clever in our new house… or maybe Mr Perkins could come and live with us," but as they looked about Mr Perkins was gone.

District Judges Laura Stolinska and Petunia Partington were drinking coffee together in Petunia's Chambers when there was a fumbling sound at the door.

Petunia said, "Come in," but no-one did so but there was a noise again. Laura went and opened the door and Mr Perkins dashed in with a mouse between his jaws. He jumped up onto Petunia's desk and laid his catch out on the blotter.

"Yukk," said Petunia.

"It's a gift to the gods," said Laura who then proceeded to say how well she was getting on with her own cats, Bella and Donna.

"Not only do they keep the mice in check at home, but they are good company when I come in from a hard day's work. I usually end up with one on my lap and one beside me purring. Having pets can be very therapeutic," she said as she reached for a scrunch of tissues and removed the dead mouse from Petunia's blotter and put it in a bin. Mr Perkins looked a bit cross.

"Yes, having pets has had an excellent effect on Milton," said Petunia. "He seems to have taken full responsibility for his bunny and guinea pig friends. He also enjoys helping out at the rescue centre and is making friends with a brother and sister just two or three years older than him. He also got an "A" at school for making a presentation when he had to stand up in front of the class and explain 'How I spent my Sunday'."

Mr Perkins looked inscrutable, but a faint purr could be detected. Then he jumped down. In an instant he was gone. Laura sighed,

"You know," she said, "he comes and goes just like the lettering on the front of the court. The maintenance people can no more sort that one out than they can the rodent problem. I do wish he or some other moggy would move in permanently."

She went to her own Chambers for the day where she was due to hear a financial case in a divorce that morning. Thoughts of Mr Perkins disappeared from her mind. She was surprised that such a case was only listed for two and a half hours, and the papers were so thin. She had been given thirty minutes reading time. She sat down with the documents and discovered the couple had agreed everything except who should keep a Green Parakeet called Norman. "Maybe not all pets were therapeutic!" she thought as she cogitated that this was a custody case in the oddest of ways.

When the case was called on the couple concerned Millie and Michael McCall were accompanied by two rather embarrassed looking solicitors, one of whom was holding a large canvass bag which seemed to move.

With a feeling of trepidation Laura asked, "What's in there?"

The solicitor opened the bag and Norman flew out and perched on her desk.

"How on earth did you get him through security?" questioned Laura.

A voice replied, "You talking to me?" It was the parakeet.

The solicitor said, "Madam, I just told security I had evidence for a case, and he never looked."

Laura inwardly cursed security.

"Phone home?" asked the parakeet.

"Can't you at least get him to be quiet?" said Laura. "Oh, and isn't he in danger of flying away? Courts are hardly places for birds."

"Fasten seatbelts, it's going to be a bumpy ride," quipped Norman.

Millie McCall intervened. "Please, Norman... shhh..." She turned to Laura. "I'm so sorry, he has watched too many films. He won't fly away. He has never been able to get much lift. He was hatched with a defective wing."

"Why did anyone think it was a good idea to bring him?" Laura asked trying not to sound too exasperated.

The embarrassed lawyers looked even more embarrassed, and one cleared his throat.

"Judge, both our clients were so insistent..."

Laura seriously considered adjourning the whole case but instead said, "Well as long as the bird is quiet and doesn't start flapping about, he can stay where he is. But one bit of trouble and he is back in the bag and the case is adjourned, because a court is no place for a parrot."

"Go ahead, make my day," squawked Norman.

"Right, I have had enough," started Laura who was about to send everyone, particularly the parakeet, away.

"Please..." said both the McCalls. Norman appeared to put his head under his wing and settle down. Against her better judgement Laura continued with the case.

Laura indicated that there was very little evidence on the matter. The couple had shared the cost of Norman and the care of Norman. There were no children and they both were out several days a week working with a day or two a week working from home. She invited submissions from the solicitors. They were both equally convincing. She sighed,

"Didn't you try mediation?" she queried.

"Mediation, arbitration, negotiations... offers and counteroffers," said a harassed looking solicitor.

"I'm gonna make him an offer he can't refuse," squawked Norman.

"This requires the 'Judgement of Solomon'," said Laura, not entirely sure what she meant by this. "I will have to retire to think about this." She rang her buzzer for the usher, Tracey, who came fairly quickly and when pushing open the door also inadvertently let in Mr Perkins.

Mr Perkins leaped up onto the desk and tried to catch Norman who squawked out,

"Zulus, thousands of them." There was a brief encounter of wings paws and feathers.

The usher stood frozen with surprise by the doorway.

Millie McCall had jumped to her feet and quickly caught Norman who she cradled in her arms. "There, there, my baby," she said as he squawked out, "Love means never having to say you're sorry." Michael McCall just sat the whole time with his arms folded. Mr Perkins had jumped all the way up onto the Royal Crest where he could not be reached and looked down silently and enigmatically. Laura inwardly prayed he would not jump down for the next few minutes.

"I think I know who is having Norman," said Laura. "I hope I don't have to spell out the reasons why he is going home with Mrs McCall?"

Michael McCall said, "I never really wanted this. I just felt the need to make her have to come to court."

"Well, then," said Laura, "I probably don't need to give a formal judgement except it might be necessary on the subject of costs, but first we need to get the creatures out of here as soon as possible. I don't want Norman to be eaten."

Mr McCall's solicitor stood up. "Please reserve costs, Madam… It's been quite enough for one day. I think my client will have to accept he is not in a good position and will hopefully negotiate something."

His opponent said, "I think my client just wants to take Norman home, so I agree."

The parties and their lawyers stumbled out of Laura's Chambers with Norman still squawking in Millie McCall's arms. His parting shot was to look up from her arms in the direction of Mr Perkins and say, "May the force be with you."

Mr Perkins responded with a smug, "Miaow," and climbed down once everyone except Laura and the usher Tracey had left the Chambers. He stood on her desk purring. She said,

"I am not sure anyone will believe me, but you knew, didn't you?" He rubbed his head against her face.

"You somehow came on purpose and showed me what a 'Judgement of Solomon' really meant," she added to Mr Perkins. Just then Tracey came to life,

"Quite the morning, Madam," she said. "I don't think the manager is going to be very pleased with security. I will go and check that the bird is safely off the premises. I don't think the Court Manager will believe the whole story of Mr Justice Pussycat!"

Laura nodded in agreement.

Mr Perkins jumped down and disappeared through the closing door before it swung shut after the usher went out.

Chapter 9

To say Renee Rollwright was stressed was to describe her usual state of being as Court Manager of the Combined Court. Her correct description by the Court Service was 'Delivery Manager' which in her view made her sound like a pizza delivery driver. There was always something going wrong. If it wasn't a judge going sick, it was the parlous state of the building. It was so embarrassing that the contractors could not even get the lettering correct. Now the security men had proved useless; so sloppy that they had let a live parakeet into the building. It was a good thing it wasn't drugs, a weapon or even a bomb.

After complaints to her manager and to her manager's manager the Court Service had finally decided to use an entirely different company to fix the lettering. They were not available immediately, so she would just have to hope that in the meantime the whole thing did not come crashing down. Then there was the rodent infestation. The only thing that had proved effective was the occasional visits of a stray moggy. She had at last gained approval for a small budget to use a local pest control man. The pub next door gave her a good report of a man they used whose van she had seen parked next to the pub. Its signage declared "Gus's Removal of Pests and

Environmental Services". She had obtained a card which had shortened the title to "GROPES" which seemed a little unfortunate. However, the proprietor Mr Gus Strong sounded very pleasant when she phoned him.

Early today she met Gus Strong for the first time. He had a quiet confidence about him and inspected all the areas of rodent activity without rush or fuss. He put a number of locked rat boxes in strategic places in the car park and different types of locked containers hidden away in the court building. She told him about the feline visitor.

"I do like cats," he said, "but the problem you have is not going to be fixed by one cat coming now and again."

She tended to agree although she had noted that the human beings with a few exceptions seemed to respond well to the odd feline visit.

"You might be surprised how much I know about cats," he added. "It's because my wife helps out at the Cat Rescue Centre, and we foster cats at home. My customers seem to enjoy their cats' companionship rather than rely on them for rodent control."

Pre-covid there was publicity for a handful of schemes for emotional support animals to be brought to court and calm people in waiting areas. If someone had a registered assistance dog the animal must be allowed into the building. The stray cat was not covered by the rules. Her own beautiful cat Luna tended to have a somewhat lonely life at home since she was out at work and her adult daughter who lived with her was busy with her own job as a physiotherapist. She had had an amicable divorce years ago. She sat in her little office and was surprised to look down and see Mr Perkins sitting beside her.

"Miaow," he said.

"Hello," she replied and scratched him behind the ears. She thought of a plan.

First, she would bring her own well-behaved cat into the building on some Family Court days and see how it went. If asked by her managers, she would say she was on the way to a vet's appointment. If it went well, she would then seek official approval to have her present on some days as a support animal. She would also contact an emotional assistance dogs' organisation and see if they would like to think up a scheme for support dogs to be brought to court from time to time. She put her hand out to stroke Mr Perkins again, but he had gone. Indeed, on later occasions if asked she would say this was the last time she could recall seeing Mr Perkins.

District Judge Roger Shadow was on one of his two-day stints visiting the court. He was thinking about how well the acquisition of a mobility scooter had gone for his wife. She had taken a cautious approach of which he approved but he was really pleased to hear how Sarah had easily mastered the very short trip to the village shop where she had bought a magazine and a carton of milk. She had told him with obvious pleasure that the Church Hall was nearby, and she would find out if there were any functions which would be practical to attend but would consult with him first. There was, for example, a local history society which met monthly and had talks on subjects relating to the history and archaeology of the area. He mused that he could no doubt sit at home once a month with his papers for court and be on hand for the girls if it meant Sarah could have an interest outside the home.

Cassie and Diana were doing very well with British Sign Language and when he had time, he went online to get more of the basics. They made a point of going to the day centre as they now had a number of friends there with whom they could often communicate and socialise. There was one young girl, Tasha, who was fairly new to signing who was an artist and they were fascinated when she brought artistic items to show them. She brought a pottery sculpture of a cat one day who she indicated visited her mother's guest house. The model looked rather familiar to Roger.

Roger had decided to go to the dog rehoming centre this coming weekend and regarded this with pleasant anticipation. The usher interrupted his thoughts to let him know the parties to his first case were in the building. It was a father and son. The dad was applying to take some of his son's accident compensation money out of court to take his son swimming with dolphins in Florida. Roger was concerned as to whether this would be a good use of the money. But first Mr Perkins appeared and jumped on his desk so he could not look at his laptop or his papers.

The cat purred and stared at him straight into his eyes. Roger found himself smiling.

"Are you trying to give me instruction?" he found himself speaking to the cat.

"Miaow," said Mr Perkins.

"Duly noted," said Roger as if he was speaking to a person and thinking of the importance of pets and other animals in people's lives. The cat jumped down and headed for the door with its tail sticking straight up like a mast.

"Goodbye then," he found himself saying.

Frankie Clancy came into his Chambers in his wheelchair guided by his father Geoffrey. Roger was initially reminded of his own daughters. Frankie was a child of twelve with a most disarming smile, Frankie had suffered more than most children of his age. A minor accident at his Primary School when he was five when a concrete roof had collapsed on him in the toilets had placed him on the operating table under general anaesthetic to repair multiple fractures in his shoulder, but the anaesthetist and his colleague had sadly made mistakes causing the child neurological damage which affected his co-ordination and thus impaired his mobility. The claims against the education authority and the hospital had just been settled last year. Whereas in the past Roger would have been inclined to say "no" from the outset to a payment out for the purposes of what might just be a nice holiday, now he was inclined to probe further.

After introductions he asked Geoffrey, "Who will go on this trip?"

The reply was, "Just me and Frankie... His mum will stay behind to look after the rest of the family."

"How long is the trip and how much of it involves swimming with dolphins?" probed Roger.

"It will be about nine days including the travel. The accommodation is wheelchair friendly so for the first couple of days Frankie can acclimatise and recover from the journey. Then maybe we might visit an aquarium. Then

Frankie will spend a day being prepared for his dolphin encounter followed by the dolphin encounter next day. It will then be up to my son if he wants to take in a theme park or so before we come home," said Geoffrey.

"How will this benefit Frankie?" asked Roger.

Geoffrey produced letters from the child's general practitioner and his school both of whom saw psychological benefits to Frankie who they indicated was bright, but frequently frustrated and depressed by his condition.

"What do think about the idea, Frankie?" asked Roger.

"I think it's brill," he said. "I want to be a marine biologist when I grow up. Not only does Florida have excellent aquariums and marine facilities but they have a number of centres with dolphins."

"I hear you are doing well at school, how will this trip impact on your studies?" asked Roger.

"Well," said Frankie, "we can go in the holidays, maybe October or February half term so I would miss very little school. But I think I can also make it into a science project. We are encouraged to use outside activities for school projects. Other boys do projects about football or maybe joining the scouts… but I have not really been able to compete. I can walk a little bit, but the other kids laugh at the way I move. Mum and Dad do kind things so I can join in holidays, like we went to a villa in Spain with a pool last year and I was able to swim in the pool, but I want to do more… I want to study the sea creatures."

Roger said, "Have you been to any aquariums already?"

"Oh yes," was the reply. "A couple. I was in a tunnel under the shark tank at one. The other had some funny penguins."

"Do you have any favourite aquatic creatures?" Roger continued to probe.

"Dad let me have a big fishtank at home and I have a big catfish I call Big Banana, but I am very interested in bottle nose dolphins and killer whales," came the response.

Roger looked at the amount which was to be taken out of the child's fund. It seemed very modest in the circumstances. He indicated his approval to the application. Thoughts of his own daughters crossed his mind. While their difficulties were multiple, nonetheless, he felt more determined than ever to acquire a dog. If he could add as many layers of interest as possible to their lives, it could only be for the good. He undertook the rest of his morning list with enthusiasm and at lunchtime approached the judges' dining room with thoughts of actually socialising with his colleagues. He had even nipped out and bought a packet of biscuits to offer people.

Today he was pleased to see His Honour Judge Stanley D'Artagnon KC, His Honour Judge Hassan Shah KC and District Judge Nick Blyton.

"Afternoon, Roger," said Nick cautiously.

"Ginger nut anyone?" said Roger not used to being sociable.

Stanley D'Artagnon KC smiled and retorted, "I could answer that in a number of ways... but I'm going to say, 'yes please'."

"It's good to see you," said Hassan Shah KC trying to smooth matters over. "Thank you for the offer."

There was some good-humoured chatter. His Honour Judge Shah KC said to Nick,

"I hear you are finally getting into your house very shortly."

"Yes," said Nick, "I can't wait. The people at the B & B are very nice but it's not the same as having your family around you and being in your own house. I shall enjoy taking my dog Jasper for walkies too... Although I will miss Mr Perkins. Mind you my daughter Maria wants us to have a cat of our own."

"I am going to get a dog," said Roger suddenly. "I am going to the dogs' home on Saturday, and I hope I can get one of those three brothers on the leaflet which was wafted around recently."

"Really?" said Stanley D'Artagnon sounding surprised. "I want one too. I am going on Saturday."

Hassan Shah KC started to laugh.

"It's a good thing there are plenty of dogs needing a home or it might be pistols at dawn!"

There were smiles all around.

"I want to get outside more," said Roger. "I am prepared to do the training. I think a dog may be good for my wife and daughters too."

"I want to do dog walks for the sake of my health," said Stanley.

Roger and Stanley had a chat about their general hopes for getting dogs.

"Why don't you go together?" said Hassan Shah KC.

They agreed they would seriously consider that suggestion. Although Roger was not used to sharing interests with other judges a few emails later and they had agreed they would meet at 'Terry Dean's Dog Rescue' at eleven o'clock on Saturday.

That fine Saturday morning three men drove into the car park of 'Terry Dean's Dog Rescue' shortly before eleven in the morning. The three men were Roger, Stanley and Dylan Jones the vet. The rehoming centre was approached down a country lane through some woods and was in effect in a large clearing in the woods, complete with an exercise field, kennels and runs, a shop for pet goods, staff restrooms and a reception and waiting area. The three men sat down, and Roger and Stanley spoke quietly together.

"I want to do everything properly," said Roger. "I shall want to register with a good vet to make sure the dog has all his health checks."

Stanley said, "Likewise. I don't know any vets but I'm sure they can recommend someone."

Dylan Jones cleared his throat. "I'm a vet," he said.

"Are you here to treat a dog?" asked Stanley.

"Not this time, although I have been a volunteer vet here," laughed Dylan. "I am here to get a dog I hope."

After a few minutes they realised that they were after the three brothers. Dylan said,

"What do you two do for a living. I assume you are colleagues…"

"We are in the legal profession," said Stanley vaguely.

"Is that right," said Dylan. "I guess I am sort of here indirectly through a legal connection… a cat who visits "The Judges' Lodgings B & B". It's a long story but it all seems to relate back to this stray cat nicknamed Mr Perkins…"

"Mr Perkins?" said Roger and Stanley together. "A black cat with yellow eyes?"

"Yes," said Dylan. "Why?"

"Mr Perkins has visited our court many times," said Stanley. "I think he is somehow responsible for me being here in an indirect way."

"And me too," said Roger. "Do we know who owns him?"

Dylan responded, "We haven't traced anyone. Vicky Poletree who owns the "The Judges' Lodgings B & B" was prepared to take him on I know. Recently I understood he has been a bit more elusive. Mind, it's a nice spot there, next to the park."

At that point two members of staff came into the room. The two women smartly dressed in green overalls smiled and one woman who had a badge saying 'Manager, Shirley' said,

"Our three candidates for the three brothers. Do you mind meeting them together?"

No-one minded. The two women took details from the three men although when addressing Dylan, she evidently knew him. Shirley jokingly said, "We hope you know what you are doing with a dog. Seeing as you are a vet!"

The three brothers who went by the names of Bob, Bing and Sammy were in three runs outside their three neighbouring kennels. They were three middle-sized brown, smooth haired dogs of no discernible breed. There was a great deal of woofing and tail wagging.

Shirley said, "We have put them in separate kennels since they are boys who are not yet neutered… I am not sure they would fight at all because they just seem playful together. Once we have had some introductions why don't we all go walkies around the exercise field?"

Shirley and her colleague brought the dogs out on leads.

The energetic dogs took the two judges and the vet for a walk. Stanley was towed along by a very lively Bob, Dylan was pulled along by busy Bing and Roger was hauled about by the slightly less bouncy Sammy. After walkies, the three men and Shirley sat on some benches with the dogs bouncing around them, having a few dog treats.

"First, these dogs need training as well as neutering," said Shirley as the dogs began to settle a little. Sammy was sitting at Roger's feet licking Roger's shoes. Bing was sitting upright and nudging Dylan. Bob was pulling on his lead and trying to pull Stanley out of his seat, presumably for further walkies. Shirley added, "If you wish to adopt, we can also sign you and your dog up for obedience class here at the centre."

"Count me in," said Dylan as his new pal looked him in the eyes.

Bob was now rolling on his back having his tummy tickled by Stanley who said, "Me too."

Sammy was gazing adoringly at Roger who was gazing back at his new doggy friend.

"How could I turn him down?" he said. "Those sad eyes."

The dogs were returned to their kennels temporarily. Shirley indicated there were formalities to complete. The dogs would be vaccinated, health checked, and their chips updated. Appointments would be sourced for neutering in due course. The three men were expected to visit their new dog at least twice over the next ten days, pay a donation to the charity and prove they had got the right equipment for their new pal, before they could take their friend home.

The dogs gazed wistfully out of the gates to their runs.

"I feel bad at leaving Bing," said Dylan.

"It is only for a few days," said Shirley.

They all sat together completing the paperwork.

"Right, I have everything I need," said Shirley getting up. "Nice to have met you all. I have signed the three of you up for the same obedience class. See you soon!"

"I was thinking," said Dylan to Stanley and Roger, "we might also regularly meet for dog-walks so the brothers might see each other. I think I can persuade Vicky at "The Judges' Lodgings" to let us start and finish dog walks there… and serve us coffee."

"What a good idea!" said Roger.

"Sounds an excellent thought," added Stanley before they all went their separate ways.

When Roger reached home Sarah was so pleased to see him in a buoyant mood.

"Are you sure we can cope?" she asked. He told her about the dog training and the proposed dog walking arrangement.

"He is the quietest of the three brothers. There was just something about him which makes me think he will fit right in," he added with confidence.

Chapter 10

The weeks which followed Roger's trip to 'Terry Dean's Rehoming Centre' saw Sarah going out on her mobility scooter with increasing confidence and joining the local historical society. Sammy the dog moved into the household. Although there were a few teething problems, now he was one of the family.

On his first night Sammy somehow slipped out of an open door and Sarah spotted a shivering scared dog out of the front window, so he was quickly retrieved. A comfortable dog bed had been placed in the kitchen but despite best endeavours Sammy seemed unable to settle shut in the kitchen and howled like a miserable upset wolf. As soon as the kitchen door was opened, he shot upstairs to the master bedroom, passing the stairlift at the speed of light.

"We should not let him sleep on our bed," said Roger thoughtfully. "With your issues, Sarah, I can't see how we can cope with a mutt on our bed."

Sarah reluctantly agreed that he was right. However, Roger pulled a spare duvet out of the linen cupboard and put it on the floor folded in two just at the foot of their bed. Sammy immediately took to this. The howling stopped. He slept at the bottom of the bed on the floor guarding his master and mistress, although in the daytime he could often be found sitting next to Cassie and Diana looking at them adoringly. Now and again, he sneaked into Roger and Sarah's bedroom during the daytime and took a crafty nap in the middle of their bed. Roger and Sarah were not sure medical people would approve on hygiene grounds, but they just laughed at the issue.

Roger found himself persevering with dealing with doggy problems such as a couple of holes being dug in the lawn and some of his socks being stolen and buried in the garden. He wondered where he had acquired his tolerance for rawhide bones being left in front of his favourite armchair or occasionally in the middle of it. Cassie and Diana loved the presence of Sammy and giggled when he stole their father's socks and came dashing into their room tossing them in the air. Recently they had a friend from the Day Centre for tea, Tasha, who attended British Sign Language classes.

It was a bit of a departure for Cassie and Diana to entertain, but Tasha transpired to be the daughter of Vicky from "The Judges' Lodgings B & B". Her mother dropped her over to the house. It seemed Tasha was trying to widen her horizons. She was taking tentative steps to have an assistance dog and wanted to see how Cassie and Diana were getting on with having a dog in the house. A cheerful afternoon of tea and cake was had by all including Sammy. When Vicky came to collect Tasha, she asked Roger if he was coming over next Saturday. He looked puzzled initially.

"The dog walking get-together organised by Dylan?" she said.

"Of course," said Roger, "with the girls having such a good time it had slipped my mind."

Dylan and Bing were for the most part inseparable. Bing sat with the reception staff or with Cleo while Dylan tended his patients. Dylan and Bing enjoyed lengthy walks together which often brought them to visit Vicky Poletree. Dylan would sit and have coffee with Vicky with Bing at their feet. If she was not too busy, they would go for a long walk in the park. On a nice day Dylan would bring with him a rug, and a picnic basket with tasty nibbles and a bottle of wine. One day they were lounging on a rug under a horse chestnut tree. Vicky was telling him how her late husband Jim used to have a dog when she first met him, and how she enjoyed the presence of dogs as well as cats. She mentioned that her daughter Tasha having finished a recent project of a cat sculpture of Mr Perkins was gradually having introductions and training with an assistance dog. She also mentioned how she had had a guest Nick who had brought his dog Jasper with him when he was in the process of moving house.

"You know, I think he is a colleague of Roger and Stanley who have Bing's brothers," said Dylan. "The obedience classes are due to finish soon I wonder if I should hurry up and set up a dog walking club… maybe meeting on Saturdays."

"What a good idea," said Vicky. "They could start and finish at the "Judges' Lodgings", and I could provide coffee and biscuits in the conservatory or the garden!"

"What about the cats?" asked Dylan.

"Tasha's little cats stick mainly to her studio, and I would imagine she would have the assistance dog in public places to give her confidence, and maybe her bedroom," replied Vicky. "As for Mr Perkins he is a law unto himself and recently he hasn't been around so much. I just have his sculpture in reception rather than the cat these days."

So that was how the Saturday dog walking club started.

Stanley was also delighted with the idea of a club to go walkies. He had been enjoying the obedience classes with Bob. Although he occasionally did play a round of golf he was spending much less time in the clubhouse. He was spending more time in the garden either with Bob the dog or with Clifford or with both. He did not enjoy shovelling up Bob's deposits on the lawn, but he had come to enjoy making the garden a fun place for both young dog and tiny tot. In the evenings he no longer found the need to swill down alcohol as if it was cola, but he would sit on the patio and drink a glass of a good vintage with appreciation, pausing to throw dog frisbees for his canine pal.

Vicky contacted Nick Blyton who was pleased to bring red setter Jasper and his son Harry along. He looked forward to seeing his former lodgings again. His family were settling down into their new home and he was pleased to get to know his colleagues better. He suggested to Stanley that they asked Bernard Woldborough to join them as well. Stanley indicated that he thought this was an excellent idea and so Bernard and his mastiff Beast were invited to join them.

So, the dog-walking club started with the three mutts who were brothers and their people, Jasper with Nick and Harry and Beast with his master Bernard. Beast was rather large but in temperament was the opposite of a beast. He was big, slobbery and lollopy. He shyly rubbed noses with Jasper while the other three hounds bounded around Vicky's Garden. Soon the dogs were all able to let off steam in the park and after energetic walkies the dogs and their masters flopped down with exhaustion in the conservatory. The dogs had bowls of water and their people enjoyed coffee, fruit juices and biscuits. Nick momentarily thought he saw a black cat and a pair of yellow eyes peering at him in reception when he walked through to the gentlemen's toilet. He felt he owed Mr Perkins a debt for helping him settle into his new job, and wanted to fuss him, and tell him he was a fine cat, but when he came out of the toilets all he could see was the sculpture of Mr Perkins.

Dylan went to pay Vicky for the refreshments in the bar, but she seemed reluctant to accept payment.

"They can afford it," said Dylan. "Everyone is very happy with the arrangement."

"If you are sure?" said Vicky working the till, "By the way, are we still going to go on any picnics?"

"Of course we are," smiled Dylan. "And when you have cover for the guesthouse, I want to take you out for dinner… and the cinema too. Proper dates."

Vicky giggled. "Not improper dates?"

"That comes later!" laughed Dylan quietly.

And so, the dog walking club and dates with Dylan became a regular feature for Vicky. Cleo sometimes minded the guesthouse sitting contentedly with a mountain of books to further her studies in animal health. She felt she could fulfil an aim to be a fully qualified veterinary nurse.

At the court Gus Strong and his van were now regular visitors and Renee not only found him effective with getting the rodents under control but enjoyed a quick natter with him when he dropped into the building. He had recently invited her to have Sunday tea with his wife and himself so that she could find out more about fostering cats from her. He said, "There are sadly so many cats who could do with a roof over their head. When my wife is not nagging me to change the letters on my cards, she is telling me to drum up support for the cat charity. I tell her the cards attract attention to my business and I do my best for the moggies."

Renee also enjoyed the odd occasion when she brought her own cat into the building as a support animal. The letters had stayed in place this time on the front of the court. The roof was not leaking anywhere. Things were going well for once.

Nick Blyton stood outside the court and thought how time had flown by. His wife and family were settled. He felt at home in his surroundings and that he really belonged here. He looked up at the gold letters which glinted in the sunshine and read "Combined Court". He entered the building. The buckets had gone, and the roof was apparently fixed. There was to be a meeting of all local judges this morning in the judges' dining room to discuss resources and sitting patterns so he was pleased to see all his colleagues there, even if some would usually sit elsewhere.

He sat down when he reached the dining room alongside District Judges Petunia Partington and Laura Stolinska. They were soon joined by Roger Shadow who smiled affably. His Honour Judge Bernard Woldborough and His Honour Judge Stanley D'Artagnon KC sat opposite, and His Honour Judge Hassan Shah KC chaired the meeting as they sipped their coffees.

"Right," said Hassan Shah, "I know at least two of you are due in other courts away from here at about half ten or eleven o'clock, so I will try to keep the meeting very short."

They quickly discussed if the courtrooms and chambers were being used in the most appropriate way from a judicial point of view and whether they were lacking the support they needed. Roger said,

"Well, the roof is fixed, and we are not inundated with mice and rats anymore. Clearly the District Judges would welcome more administrative support, but things are better than they used to be in the past."

"You seem more upbeat," said Petunia.

"I am," said Roger. "I welcome the idea of support animals for people coming to court. Whilst not everyone likes animals, many people can benefit."

They all agreed such schemes were welcome and they would support such schemes and would arrange a specific meeting with Renee to discuss it. The meeting broke up and Stanley said,

"You know it was that black cat with the yellow eyes which started all this about support animals."

"Indeed it was," said Petunia. "You know, I haven't seen Mr Perkins for a while. I'd like to think he has found his home. I feel I owe him a debt."

Laura said, "Yes... me too. I think that it is due to him I have my two lovely cats."

The other judges nodded in agreement to the sentiment and then went about the day's work. Morale was good and they all were thankful to have met the black cat with the yellow eyes, but their minds were on their work, their families and their own pets.

Back at "The Judges' Lodgings B & B", Vicky also shared the opinion that she owed a debt to Mr Perkins, but he was nowhere to be seen. Life was good. Tasha now had the support of Springer Spaniel, Nelson. He had recently moved in and thus far everything was progressing very well. Tasha had also signed up to start a Foundation Degree at the University Technical College in town, to start in a few months' time. Having Nelson had made her much more independent although she was keen to continue with classes to improve her British Sign Language. With the support of Nelson, she had also taken a bus to go and have tea with Cassie and Diana. Since both Nelson and Sammy were well-trained in their own ways there were no doggy issues when Sarah showed her into the house.

Vicky looked forward to her next date with Dylan, although next time she would see him would be for the dog walking club on Saturday. She was delighted that Cleo was still finding the time to help at the guesthouse enabling her to go on dates with Dylan. Cleo indeed looked very content with her situation.

That Saturday morning Vicky glanced at her computer. There was an email from Herbie Greystock which said,

"Hi Vicky,

I hope you are well. Reuben and I just wanted to thank you and Mr Perkins the cat for your kindness and help during our visit. It was great to find out about my ancestors but also Reuban and I discovered we had a common liking for cats! So, I have moved address.

Reuben and I have bought a little house together in a leafy suburb of Chicago. No more apartment living for us. We initially thought we would maybe just have a couple of cats which is partly why we bought the house. Well things did not work out quite as intended.

We went to the Cat Shelter and there was mom cat with three little kittens. They had re-homed three other kittens, but she still had three, so we decided to take the family. Minnie is a pretty white cat with black patches and her kittens, Patches, Missy and Tiny have similar markings. We had a 'Catio' built in our yard since Reuben felt she might stray to the freeway, and Minnie and her kittens seemed real happy. In case you didn't know a catio is a kind of mesh enclosure around part of a yard to make a safe space for one's cats.

One day, however, there was a sad mewing from the yard, just outside the catio, and we found a very skinny ginger cat pathetically scratching to get inside our place. That turned out to be Lyon. We don't know where he came from, and no-one claimed him so now he lives with us as well. Incredibly our cat family are all friends.

I guess we won't be going overseas for a while now, but Reuben and I are very happy living with our cat family. I guess we owe it to that cat Mr Perkins. I have hardly had any time to look at my ancestor research.

Reuben has a friend Ray who has a wooden vacation cabin just in Indiana by the lakeshore, amongst the dunes, so I guess we might try to take the cats on our next vacation although I am nervous of having a car full of crying cats on the expressway. We shall just have to see.

Please let us know how you all are.

With grateful thanks,

Herbie Greystock".

Vicky was sure Tasha would be most interested in this news, but her musing upon it was interrupted by a cacophony of noise as the dog walking club burst into reception. There was a brief hiatus as Bob, Bing and Sammy became entangled with their leads twisted and joyous woofing. The statue of Mr Perkins fell off the windowsill with a thump. Vicky picked it up and noted there was some minor damage, with the tail having been chipped off and one ear being cracked.

Tasha appeared with Nelson and Vicky pointed out the damage.

"It's a bit of a shame," said Tasha, not sounding too upset. "I will put it away in the cupboard. I was thinking of sculpting Trigg and Sif... or perhaps Nelson."

She changed the subject. "I think you have help from Cleo today so if it's okay I am off with Nelson to take the bus to visit Cassie and Diana?"

Vicky indicated that she was quite content for Tasha to go out and helped her move the broken statue to a cupboard. She would tell her all about Herbie's email later.

There was cheerful banter going on in the conservatory. Dylan said,

"It's been a lovely morning; the dogs have really enjoyed themselves."

"I think the humans have enjoyed themselves too. Life can be good," said Roger.

"Indeed," said Stanley. "I have been enjoying it just now. Having the dog so much improves things."

"I'll drink to that," said Roger raising his coffee cup in a mock toast, "and to that cat Mr Perkins, wherever he is, who I think showed me the way."

Epilogue

A black cat with yellow eyes climbed one of the hills just outside the city. The wind got up and the breeze rippled his fur. There was a determination in his walk. He reached the top of the hill and looked back with a wistful, almost longing gaze. His expression told a story of work having been done. After one last long look, he strode purposefully down the other side of the hill into some woods where he disappeared into the shadows.

A Cat's Judgement

Information from Mr Perkins
Of Courts and Judges

HM Court and Tribunal Service is the body responsible for administering Courts in England and Wales

(https://www.gov.uk/government/organisations/hm-courts-and-tribunals-service/about)

About 19,000 people are employed by HMCTS. When the county court system was created as a result of the County Courts Act 1846 (9 & 10 Vict. c. 95), there were 491 county courts in England and Wales but the court locations have been considerably reduced. Since the Crime and Courts Act 2013 came into force, there has been one unified County Court, sitting simultaneously in many different locations. The number of court buildings in England and Wales reduced considerably since 2015 but there are still many locations with buildings housing multiple jurisdictions of crime, family and civil work, often referred to as Combined Courts.

As of 1 April 2023, there were 3483 judges holding judicial appointments in England and Wales. They were appointed by the Judicial Appointments Commission.

https://www.gov.uk/government/statistics/diversity-of-the-judiciary-2023-statistics/diversity-of-the-judiciary-legal-professions-new-appointments-and-current-post-holders-2023-statistics.

There are different types of judges in England and Wales with a distinct hierarchy. This is explained by the Judicial Appointments Commission. https://judicialappointments.gov.uk/what-it-is-like-to-be-a-judge/.

Suffice it to say that a Civil and Family District Judge has a very broad jurisdiction, but appeal from their decisions often lies to a Circuit Judge. Just one final sentence about judges; they are human beings too!

Assistance and Support Animals

The Equality Act 2010 section 173 defines assistance animals (dogs) to whom legal discrimination laws apply. Under the Equality Act 2010, users of assistance dogs have a right not to be discriminated against based on their disability. There is no such legal protection relating to emotional support animals. Assistance dogs are defined as dogs trained to guide a blind person, dogs trained to guide a deaf person, dogs trained by certain charities to assist someone with a disability and dogs trained to assist people with certain prescribed disabilities.

"Guide dogs" https://www.guidedogs.org.uk/about-us/   is a well-known charity which devotes its resources to providing guide dogs for blind people. It says,

"We're a charity, almost entirely funded by donations, and we are the world's largest assistance dog organisation. As world leaders in puppy socialisation and dog training, we're the only organisation to breed and train guide dogs in the UK."

"Hearing dogs for deaf people" https://www.hearingdogs.org.uk/about/ train intelligent dogs to aid deaf people, from hearing a smoke alarm to hearing a baby's cry. Sometimes their jobs will be to reconnect with aspects of life and combat loneliness.

Assistance dogs UK https://www.assistancedogs.org.uk/ describes its functions:

"Assistance dogs are highly trained to support disabled people and people with medical conditions in a variety of ways.

Assistance Dogs UK is a coalition of assistance dog organisations that have been accredited by Assistance Dogs International (ADI) and/or The International Guide Dog Federation (IGDF).

ADUK members are non-profit organisations that work to the highest standards of assistance dog training and welfare. From guide dogs to medical alert dogs, from autism dogs to hearing dogs, our members train assistance dogs that change, and often save, the lives of their owners."

While there is not the legal protection for having an emotional support animal there are one or two charities who do support people in having emotional support animals since many would argue these animals improve quality of life and aid mental health.

Pet Rescue

As for the support of animals there are many organisations in the UK which support different aspects of the welfare of pets from the RSPCA to the PDSA and the Blue Cross.

Pre-eminent in the protection of cats in the UK is Cats' Protection. https://www.cats.org.uk/about-cp. They say,

"We help an average of 157,000 cats and kittens every year thanks in no small part to our network of over 210 volunteer-run branches and 34 centres."

It should not be forgotten that there are many smaller organisations which help cats and kittens. Fortunately, there are people who love cats and kittens in most cities and villages. For example, in a village in North Lincolnshire is Burton on Stather Cat Rescue. Organisations such as this are listed on a website known as Cat Chat.

https://www.catchat.org/shelter_centre/index.php?route=shelters/shelter&path=202burton-upon-stather&page=1&section=2.

In the USA media personality Jackson Galaxy has done much to publicise cat rescue https://bestfriends.org/partners/jackson-galaxy-foundation and there are many different organisations and countless websites.

Cat and dog rescue is a much needed international phenomenon with rescue organisations in all types of places, even small islands, for example Cats in Need Menorca

https://catsinneedmenorca.org/#:~:text=Founded%20by%20Janice%20B ockling%2C%20Cats,cats%20in%20Menorca%20since%201999..

In the UK, the Dog's Trust is the largest charity rehoming and rescuing dogs. https://www.dogstrust.org.uk/.

There are of course many other dog rescue charities in the UK, a good example being Jerry Green Dog Rescue https://www.jerrygreendogs.org.uk.

This charity operates in Lincolnshire, Nottinghamshire and South Yorkshire and has been operating since 1961.

There are of course rabbit and guinea pig rescue charities such as Scunthorpe Rabbit Rescue and there are details on the Rabbit Rehome website. http://www.rabbitrehome.org.uk/rescue.asp?Rescue=557.

British Sign Language and the Deaf Community

British Sign Language is said to be the fourth indigenous language of the British Isles after English, Welsh and Scots Gaelic. It is used by about 90,000 deaf people as their preferred first language. Much information can be gleaned from the National Deaf Children's Society.

https://www.ndcs.org.uk/information-and-support/language-and-communication/sign-language/learning-bsl/

Interesting insights into the deaf community and the use of British Sign Language can be gleaned from the Limping Chicken, an independently run blog.

https://limpingchicken.com/about/.

An important message in the website Deaf Mosaic https://deaf-mosaic.com/ is that with the right support deaf people can do anything.

Stephen Iliffe's Deaf Mosaic says:

"Stephen's Deaf Mosaic challenges the general public to understand it is not deafness that disables people, but the barriers in hearing society that often frustrates our dreams."

Stephen illustrates the point himself with his own photography.

If I have got any information wrong about BSL, deaf people and their active community I hope they will forgive me.

Acknowledgements

And a message from Mr Perkins

I would like to thank my cousin Emma Iliffe for all the information she has given me on British Sign Language. Emma is a leading light in the teaching of BSL, a language which is the main language for so many. Any mistakes I may have made in respect of BSL, and the deaf community will be entirely mine.

I would like to thank Burton on Stather Cat Rescue for letting my husband and I adopt our most recent cats. I would like to thank our cat Tom for being the model and/or inspiration for the drawings of Mr Perkins. He was originally rescued with his brother Charlie by Cats' Protection.

This book is intended to be a work of fiction. No-one says you have to get a dog or a cat if it doesn't suit you. No-one says all dogs and cats are well behaved either. Sadly, some dogs are not suitable to be family pets let alone assistance animals, and some people have allergies to some pet fur. You don't have to learn British Sign Language or get a dog or a cat or a rabbit or indeed acquire any information or insight from Mr Perkins' adventures. But if you do meet Mr Perkins, he probably does have something important to say to you even if it is only "Miaow". He may give you a few purrs if you give him some cat treats. He is after all just a stray black cat with yellow eyes; isn't he?

Information about

Suzanne Stephenson and her books

I would like to thank you for taking the time to read my books. If you have a moment to spare to review the book you have been reading, I would appreciate it. You may have your own thoughts about what I have written and that is fine. I was a lawyer for many years and then a District Judge. Any legal background is inspired by my long legal career although I hasten to stress the fictional nature of the humans. I am also privileged to live in the English countryside, surrounded by animals who provide a lot of inspiration, as did the bear I saw on holiday in Canada who sparked off the ideas for "Bearswood End". I enjoy sketching and the animal pictures are often sketches of animals around the farm. I sometimes think the animals are in charge.

I want to give particular thanks to Sarah Luddington from Mirador Publishing who took me and the animal inspired books under her wing.

If you want to contact me, please feel free to look at my Instagram page:

Suzanne Stephenson (@bearswood_end).

Or contact me through the website:

https://stephensons-authors.co.uk/

Email address: adventures@stephensons-authors.co.uk

The following are books I have written:

Bearswood End

A scientist wanders out into the wilderness and finds a mysterious village populated by bears. To be accurate the bears find him. Can the secret village of the bears survive a threat from the outside world? Read the scientist's diary and the story of the woman who finds it.

Mr Perkins takes Charge

A black cat walks into a solicitors' office. Lives change of the lawyers and people who cross this cat's path, usually for the better. Is he just a stray cat and is it all a coincidence or is there something more mysterious afoot? If you like cats, you may find this intriguing. If you are just curious about the goings-on of a lawyers' office satisfy your curiosity following the trail of sunshine left by Mr Perkins' paws.

Waste

This is a legal satire about activities at a Combined Court in a fictional northern town. Two young people arrive whose lives might otherwise have gone to waste and make fresh starts in this fictional town which boasts as main industries a waste plant and a sausage factory. Meet the judges, MPs and other local characters.

Forever Waste

More goings-on within Waste encompassing a Romcom and sequels to the original book. You will find romance against the background of the court, its lawyers and judges and this northern city and its politicians, and there is even an election in the city. You will also understand the highs and lows of the local football club, and you may even decide to copy a few recipes.

The World According to Patrick White

This is a comic tale with a pinch of satire about a lawyer who finds she has a talking pig, and we discover how he sees the human world and what he thinks of some of our habits and human foibles. Find out how the lawyer and her family cope with this pig of a situation. Needless to say, pig and human have a few adventures before the tale is over, including a court case where the pig is an expert witness and an encounter with a Royal dignitary.

Printed in Great Britain
by Amazon

43562829R00069